"Where I Want You,"

he murmured, his mouth close to her ear. "You can't run away from me here."

"Are you going to do something to make me want to run?" she asked, trying to sound light. She was too conscious of his warm breath on her lips as he lowered his head. "What are you doing?"

"The better to hear you with, my dear. My, what big eyes you have." His eyes gleamed with mischief.

"So you've read 'Little Red Riding Hood,' huh?"

"I was a kid once, you know, and little boys read fairy tales, too."

"I'll just bet the wolf was your favorite character."

"Now why do you say that?" he asked. "Are you afraid I want to gobble you up?"

BARBARA CAMERON

says fiction has always been her first love, although she began writing professionally as a reporter. Combining her "vivid imagination" with an addiction for people watching, she creates warm, believable stories about men and women in love. Her interests include reading, travel and protecting the environment, especially the state in which she lives, Florida.

Dear Reader:

SILHOUETTE DESIRE is an exciting new line of contemporary romances from Silhouette Books. During the past year, many Silhouette readers have written in telling us what other types of stories they'd like to read from Silhouette, and we've kept these comments and suggestions in mind in developing SILHOUETTE DESIRE.

DESIREs feature all of the elements you like to see in a romance, plus a more sensual, provocative story. So if you want to experience all the excitement, passion and joy of falling in love, then SILHOUETTE DESIRE is for you.

Karen Solem
Editor-in-Chief
Silhouette Books

BARBARA CAMERON
Rapture
Of The Deep

Silhouette Desire
Published by Silhouette Books New York
America's Publisher of Contemporary Romance

SILHOUETTE BOOKS, a Division of Simon & Schuster, Inc.
1230 Avenue of the Americas, New York, N.Y. 10020

Distributed by Pocket Books

ISBN: 0-671-50007-4

First Silhouette Books printing September, 1984

10 9 8 7 6 5 4 3 2 1

For Rita Shell Federle:
May your dreams come true too!

1

Lori stroked through the sea, enjoying the feel of the water against her skin, warm and wonderful and delightfully soothing. This was her time—the soft glow of dawn breaking—when she was part of the earth and its creatures, awakening to the rhythm of another day. The sea mirrored the colors of the sun as it burned through the early morning mists, touching the water with opaline shimmers of pink, lavender and pearl, touching Lori's skin, too, as she swam, making her feel even more a part of the earth and the sea and the sky.

She swam for a long time, absorbing the calm she always gained from cleaving the water in strong, even strokes and from watching the sun rise in the sky and become bold and brilliant.

Lori saw something different at the dawn of a new day. Sometimes it was just a variation in the color of the sea or sky or something washed up along the sandy shore: on one day, glistening pebbles of tiny crystalline jellyfish mocked diamonds with their brilliance; on another day there were clumps of seaweed torn from their watery bed beneath the ocean depths; on still another, she saw the odd piece of driftwood polished to a pale smoothness by the action of the waves.

Today, the sand was a soft, rosy pink beneath the light of the rising sun. It was pink partly because on this east Florida beach the sand was mixed with bits of the soft reddish rock called coquina and partly because the sun seemed reluctant to do more than gleam, moon-like, through the mists. In the water, a butterfly shape that appeared green beneath the surface of the sea, a manta ray swimming to deeper waters, moved away from Lori on contact with her leg.

Things that go bump in the water, she thought with a smile, musing about how some people wouldn't swim in the sea because they feared other occupants, just as some people wouldn't walk about in the darkness. But neither frightened Lori. The darkness contained only what had been there in the daylight, the sea only those inhabitants that belonged there far more than she. The fuss those people made when they went swimming or scuba diving! thought Lori. After all, giant clams didn't lie in wait at the bottom of the sea, hoping to make dip of some hapless human who became trapped in their gaping valves; octopi didn't swim about hoping to wrap their tentacles around a swimmer in a deadly embrace. And sharks, which Jacques-Yves Cousteau called the splendid savage of the sea, were dangerous only when they confused a swimmer's motions for the thrashing of a wounded fish. They were, after all, only a perfect eating machine that had remained unchanged after thousands of years of evolution. Far from illogically fearing the predator, Lori instead had a cautious respect for it when she was in the sea.

Her musings on the shark, master of his sea domain, reminded her of Jordan Stark, the new director of the dolphin communication research facility at which Lori worked. There was something fascinating about him; the lithe animal sort of grace with which he moved, the stare as unblinking as—a shark stalking his prey. His ability to find her wherever she might be in the facility to discuss a problem was uncanny, unerring, as if he possessed some kind of sonar. Stop that, she told herself. You're just being fanciful.

Swimming in water that was turning aquamarine beneath the brightening rays of the sun, Lori reflected on how often she saw Jordan striding around the facility, jotting down notes to bring to the daily staff meetings. He'd discarded that beautifully cut gray business suit after the first day, opting for casual clothes, usually the white sport shirt printed with the aqua and sea-blue design that the staff wore, with white jeans or the many-pocketed khaki shorts that revealed bronzed, well-muscled legs.

Rumor had it there was going to be a cut in some of the special projects because of a drying-up of federal funding. Lori had the awful premonition that one of the first to go might be her pet project—working with Aphrodite, "her" dolphin, and a group of children who were victims of retardation or special learning problems. She knew all too well the criticism Jordan might voice—others had told her that teaching such children was fine, but there was only so far you could take them, and they'd never be normal, these kids, would they?

Of course, that was often said by people who also asked just how much Lori expected to learn from studying how to communicate with dolphins. "After all, they're just fish, aren't they?" a woman had asked her once. Lori had responded that dolphins were mammals, that people could learn a great deal if they just dispensed with their preconceived ideas about their supposed superiority as humans. "Dolphins can be much more than trained performers or underwater servants assisting divers," she'd gone on to explain. "Their brain size indicates they may be more intelligent than man; dolphins might be the means of opening up communication with other species. Imagine what that might mean. . . ." She'd trailed off, aware that the woman was staring at her with a rather glassy-eyed expression, realizing that she wasn't communicating in a very successful way with one of her own species.

A glimpse of silver motion caught Lori's eye, and she treaded water as she watched a school of dolphins cavort farther out in the sea. Their play was free-spirited and friendly, and at times like this, Lori found herself wishing that Aphrodite could join them, have some experience outside the tank in which she'd been born. But the dolphin might not survive out in the wild after all her years in captivity. As much as Lori and the others at the facility felt their research was humane, none of them was completely at peace with holding these intelligent creatures in captivity. Jordan had spoken of his hopes of eventually having additions to the facility constructed so that the dolphins would be free to come and go as they worked with humans.

The dolphins had distracted Lori from thinking about Jordan for a moment, but now another recurring thought, one that had been troubling Lori, surfaced: What would she do if he canceled her program when she felt as strongly about it as she did? Could she, would she, want to stay and work at some other project if that happened?

The school of dolphins moved on and disappeared from view, but Lori, lost in her thoughts, wasn't really watching now. She turned and began swimming toward shore, knowing by the position of the sun in the sky that it was time for her to be getting ready for her class with the kids. Remembering what she'd learned from the Yamamotos, the Japanese couple who ran a nearby restaurant and had become friends, Lori thought, Time will tell. You don't know what's going to happen, and worrying won't help. So far nothing had happened; maybe everything would work out. Jordan certainly seemed fair.

Her spirits were buoyant after the marvelous swim, and she lifted her face, thinking what a beautiful day it was going to be with the sky so clear and blue, the air soft and sweet after being cleansed over miles of Atlantic Ocean. Lori swung her arms as she whirled around, sending up a shower of sparkling drops in her own joyous salute to the day before she stepped through the lacy foam-capped wavelets and onto shore.

Her eyes widened as she saw him—the man she'd

just been thinking about—in the flesh, or just about. Jordan half reclined on the sand beside her towel and sweater, naked save for a brief white swimsuit that covered only a small portion of a body that was one all-over bronzed glory of manhood. Lori found her gaze traveling down his chest, which was covered with dark hair that curled in a narrowing vee to the waistband, and she abruptly dragged her eyes and thoughts upward. Jordan's elbows rested on the sand, his long legs stretched out before him. He was a study in relaxation, but his gaze was as scorching as an overhead Florida sun on tender white skin.

Lori's arms fell to her sides as she walked toward him, willing herself not to let his attention to her slender figure in a clinging blue maillot made of a satiny-type nylon disconcert her. When she reached the spot where she'd left her things, Lori stopped and bent slightly, swinging the long length of her hair to one side, grasping it and wringing out the salt water. She reached for the towel and began drying off.

"How was the water?"

"Marvelous!"

"You were out rather far for being alone, weren't you? What if you'd had some kind of trouble?"

"See that fisherman down there?" When he looked in the direction she indicated, she said, "He's retired, and comes down here every morning about the time I do. I'm sure if I had a problem he'd get help."

"And what if it didn't arrive in time?"

She didn't really know what to say. How could she explain that she'd always been a bit of a loner, and that she didn't expect help from others?

His eyes followed the direction of the towel she used, and she tried not to hurry the motion of her terry-covered hand as it slid across breasts barely covered by the suit, then down the curve of her hip and down one leg and then the other. Reaching for her sweater, she said, "If you'll excuse me, I have to get ready for my first class."

"That's what I wanted to talk to you about," he said quietly.

Lori pulled the sweater on over her head, grateful that for a moment it hid the expression of fear that passed over her face at his words; then her face emerged over the cowl neck of the pale turquoise blouson. Early spring mornings here at Aqua Vista could still be cool, so he mistook her shiver for a chill and handed her his towel, telling her to cover her legs as she sat down on her own towel.

"What is it you wanted to talk about?" she asked him.

"You know we're having some problems with funding," he began. "I have to spend what we have on programs that have the most potential for long-range success."

Lori winced. "Just because these kids won't ever be like you and me is no reason to turn our backs on them, is it? The report I submitted to you shows what tremendous gains we've made with their rate of learning and their memory retention. If you could just see . . ." That gave her an idea. "Jordan, just come to one of my classes. Then you'll see it's a project you'll want to keep. Please?" She put a hand on his arm and looked into his eyes with an earnest expression. When his own glance went to her hand, she realized what she'd done and pulled it away, telling him, "Sorry. I guess I just get a little carried away about my kids."

"You don't have any of your own?"

Lori shook her head, flipping over her shoulder the drying strands of hair she usually wore in one long golden braid that hung from the crown of her head nearly to her waist. "I'm not married. But that's getting off the subject. You wanted to talk about my project."

"Would it be terrible if we talked personally?" he inquired with a wry smile. "I'd like to get to know you."

"All my background is in my personnel file," she said a little stiffly.

"Now you're getting all prickly, like a little puffer fish."

"Don't you know it's not polite to compare someone to a silly-looking fish—"

"—that happens to be considered such an aid to male virility that Japanese men have been known to risk death from its poison by eating it?" he returned teasingly.

Lori shifted a little uncomfortably. She'd looked up several times at meetings this past week to see him staring at her with those eyes. . . . She glanced away from them now, away from hair as black as the depths of the sea where sunlight couldn't reach, to stare out at the ocean rolling onto the shore.

"I know all the statistics: Lauralee Fairchild, also known as Lori; age: thirty; place of birth: Orlando, Florida; education: master's degree in marine biology from the University of Florida; length of employment at Aqua Vista Research: five years; current project: utilization of dolphins in teaching retarded and other learning-disabled children."

Lori stared at him with unconcealed surprise. "Can you remember all that about everyone here?"

He shook his head.

"Then why . . ." she began, then stopped. There was something there, an undercurrent of something sexual in the air as their glances locked; then she pulled her gaze away.

But he wouldn't let her avoid his eyes. With one hand he gently turned her face so that she had to look at him. With his other hand he brushed back the drying golden strands of hair that billowed out in the breeze like a shimmering fan, cloaking her delicate features. "Because I wanted to know more about that elusive Lori nobody here could tell me much about, the one who seems to keep to herself and her dolphin. I was intrigued by those strange blue-green eyes of yours, aquamarine and deep as that sea out there, that air of sensitive vulnerability and almost provocative innocence about you."

"I—I have to be getting to my class," she told him, stammering a little and feeling like an awkward teen-ager as she pulled her face away, got up and reached down for her things. The thick curtains of her hair falling forward hid her expression as she reached for her towel.

But Jordan was holding the other end of it and wouldn't let go. "Say *please*," he said when she demanded that he give it to her.

"I'm not interested in playing tug of war this morning. I'm late!"

"What *are* you interested in playing?" he asked, his hold on the towel appearing to slacken as he looked up with a mischievous gleam in the depths of those black eyes.

Lori glared at him and yanked harder—and found herself landing with a thump on her bottom. "Ouch!" she cried, scrambling up onto her knees to surreptitiously rub at the part of her anatomy that smarted. "That wasn't very nice!"

"Neither were you to the person who can see that your program continues."

Her eyes widened. "Are you saying I have to . . . do something to keep it going?"

"Why don't we have dinner and discuss it?" Now that he'd released the towel, he was sitting in his former position, a lazy sprawl, resting his elbows on the sand and staring up at her stiff-backed figure looming over him.

All Lori wanted to do at that moment was kick sand in his face and see how he liked eating *that,* and threaten him with a suit for sexual harassment or something. But in the distance she could hear the happy cries of her already arrived students, could imagine their disappointment if they couldn't play and learn with their beloved dolphin. . . .

"All right, Mr. Stark," she said finally. "I'll have dinner with you."

"*Jordan.* Where's a good place around here?"

"The Sea Dragon. They serve Japanese and American food."

"Okay. Then I'll meet you at seven. I know where you live."

She raised her eyebrows in question, then remembered the personnel file. "Seven," she said shortly, turning to leave him.

There was no need for her to run over to her apartment beside the research facility for clothes; her swimsuit was her uniform for class. And no need for special materials—they were the laminated plaques kept beside the dolphin's tank. Her students and her teaching assistant were already there, getting reacquainted after the absence of their weekend apart.

"Hi, Timmy, ready for school?" she asked her four-year-old pupil. He nodded his head happily, wearing the sweet smile of the Down's Syndrome child—a child forever truly innocent. Feeling her heart turn over, as it always did with "her" kids, Lori held his chubby body against her and walked down the steps into the tank of water that picked up its aquamarine hue from the painted sides.

A gray shape moved with bulletlike speed beneath the water, then leaped from it to somersault in a spinning wheel of sleek, pearly gray body and dive back to the bottom. Then its head emerged near her hand again, prodded Timmy's hand, merry invitation on the seraphic, seemingly perpetually smiling face.

"Hi, Dee Dee!" Timmy cried with no prompting from Lori.

Chattering her high-pitched, giggly notes, cleaving her body backward in the water, the dolphin nodded her shining head, crying out her own greeting to the child and Lori.

They started the lesson: Lori would take a plaque from her assistant and show the picture on it to the child, then let him toss it to the dolphin. Aphrodite would retrieve it, swimming back with the attached

17

rope around her nose, and give it back to Timmy. After he'd correctly said the word for the picture on the plaque, he was allowed to give Aphrodite a fish.

Lori would never forget the first such lesson with a child like Timmy. The look of wonder on the little girl's face when she saw the dolphin and then petted it had been so poignant. There had been a frustrating tossing out of the plaque three times before the word had slipped from the child's lips, sounding rusty, almost as if it had been in the water too long. Lori had looked to the child's mother with triumph at finally having got the response she'd been trying for and saw the tears slipping down the woman's face. Later, after talking to the woman, Lori found out why she'd cried over her daughter's saying the word—other teaching methods had failed miserably. The memory of that day still made Lori's throat tight with emotion. Jordan couldn't cancel this program; he couldn't! she swore to herself. Not when he saw the difference it had made in the lives of children like Timmy here, and the others jumping up and down, impatiently awaiting their turn with Aphrodite.

Two hours later, the last child taken from her, as always sorry to leave but waving cheerfully and promising to be back the next day to "teach Dee Dee," Lori started to climb out of the tank. She looked up to find Jordan holding out a toweling robe to her. "How long have you been here?" she asked, sliding her arms into the robe and belting it around her waist.

"For nearly the whole lesson," he told her.

She searched his face for some sign of expression, but there was none.

"Anything else you need me to do before I go to lunch?" Betsy called. "I stacked up the plaques and gave Aphrodite the rest of the fish."

Lori shook her head. "No, thanks, Betsy, I'll see you later."

Jordan had walked over to the side of the tank and was kneeling beside it, unmindful of the dampness caused by all the splashing that went on during the lesson. Aphrodite swam over to him, extending a flipper to him. As Jordan grasped it, Lori could easily tell how he felt about the gesture of friendship from mammal to human as hand touched hand—for the flipper was a flesh-covered extension that covered a very human-shaped hand, part of the transformation the dolphins had undergone as they moved from land to sea and evolved according to the different needs of the sea environment. How Lori wished she could have as easily known his reaction to the lessons he'd witnessed.

"What's her name?"

"Aphrodite."

"The goddess of love. She's so soft," he said, caressing Aphrodite's head with his hand. "As soft as a woman's skin." As he gazed at Lori while he stroked the dolphin and the gap between them seemed to diminish. It was almost as if he were stroking *her* with his words and his hands, his gaze was so magnetic.

"It . . . sure isn't like mine," Lori said lightly, breaking the spell. Hers was a little wrinkled from all the extended exposure to the water; she couldn't wait to get some lotion on it. "What did you think of the lesson?"

He got to his feet. "I think I'll tell you that later, at dinner." Then he was gone.

"Miss Fairchild is in here," Lori heard Mrs. Yamamoto say. Then the delicate rice-paper panel was swishing open and she saw the six-foot-plus Jordan dwarfing the diminutive Japanese woman as they stood in the doorway.

"Hello," Jordan said, clearly surprised at her appearance as he entered, his feet silent on the highly polished floor in the soft slippers guests exchanged for their street shoes when they entered The Sea Dragon.

"Welcome," Lori said in Japanese. Jordan's secretary had called her an hour ago, saying his meeting had run late and asking if she'd please meet him here.

She knelt before the low table in the traditional dining posture, dressed in the floor-length kimono of aquamarine, ivory and coral-patterned silk that had been a recent gift of the Yamamotos. The Oriental garment, with its wide, flowing sleeves and gracefully wrapped style, was flattering to her figure and her glowing tan, Lori knew from the appreciative look Jordan was giving her now and the glances that had been directed her way as she entered the restaurant. True to the style of the garment, she'd twisted her hair up atop her head; chignon pins of ivory held it in place, and a comb that had also been a gift from the Yamamotos decorated the topknot, its tiny ivory bells tinkling whenever Lori moved her head.

"That's quite a metamorphosis," Jordan told her as he lowered himself to sit, Japanese fashion, on a tatami mat before the low lacquered table.

The harplike sounds of a koto filled the room; the

masculine scent of Jordan's aftershave invaded Lori's senses. They sipped sake, the Japanese rice wine, which Mrs. Yamamoto had left on the table for Lori to pour into tiny, hand-painted porcelain cups. Wine, her friend had once told her, was best when served at the same temperature as that of the human body.

At least the temperature the human body was supposed to be. Each time Jordan's thigh brushed hers . . . Why did Mrs. Yamamoto have to give us this *o-zashiki* when she has other dining rooms that aren't so small and . . . intimate just because I said a Mr. Stark would be joining me soon? Lori worried that he could feel the heat her body was generating at the contact with his.

The rice-paper panel opened, and Mrs. Yamamoto bowed politely. "Lori-*san*, are you and your guest ready to order?"

"Yes," said Lori; then she turned to Jordan, realizing she should have asked. "Would you like to order, or shall I?"

"I feel like the Westerner here, so perhaps you should," he told her wryly.

To Jordan's raised eyebrows of surprise, Lori ordered in fluent Japanese; then, nodding, Mrs. Yamamoto went to close the panel. Her warm glance of approval at Jordan and her very Western wink at Lori told Lori far better than words that Mrs. Yamamoto had deliberately given them the most intimate *o-zashiki*. If she only knew this was strictly business, thought Lori.

"I gather you come here often."

"The Yamamotos are my friends," she said simply. "They were very good to me after Joe died."

"Joe?"

"My foster father. He lived with me here at Aqua Vista for several months before he died, and we ate here a lot. He loved Japanese food." She didn't want to talk about Joe; that was too private. She wanted to talk about her project. "But you haven't told me yet what you've decided."

"Here's our food," Jordan pointed out when Mrs. Yamamoto returned bearing a tray filled with many covered dishes. "We'll talk about it after."

"But . . ." Sighing, Lori wished service hadn't been so fast. She helped him to a portion of Japanese custard soup and various dishes of vegetables and seafood prepared in the Oriental manner, as well as rice, from the loaded tray. "That's shark," she told Jordan as he glanced at the contents of one dish. "She thought you might like to try it. Unless you're squeamish, of course," she added impishly.

He looked at her as if to say, Do I look the type to be afraid of trying anything? "Seems appropriate, somehow. Man bites shark," he remarked, and Lori laughed.

The smile on Mrs. Yamamoto's wizened little face was smug as she asked, "*Hashi*, Lori?"

Lori nodded, accepting the chopsticks for both of them, waiting for Jordan to refuse them and ask for other eating utensils. Instead, Jordan took them, tearing the paper from the pair of half-split chopsticks and easily separating them. Lori felt a trifle deflated, having hoped she could disconcert him, as he did her. He started to discard the paper, then noticed the fortune printed on it in Japanese as well as English.

"What's yours say?"

"What? Oh, probably the same as yours," she said hastily, tucking the paper beside her plate on the side away from his. "Hey!" she cried when he reached across. He had the paper in his hands before she could snatch it away. He read it, and when he handed it back, his expression was enigmatic, as inscrutable as a man of the Orient.

Had it been Mama-*san's* idea of a joke—or merely coincidence? Lori wondered, taking a drink of the Japanese green tea and scalding her mouth before she realized the fragrant liquid was too hot to drink. How corny to give her—if it had been deliberate—a fortune that said *Today, you'll find a love that will be true a lifetime!* Why, the woman was as bad as—as a gypsy fortune-teller who gazed into her crystal ball and "saw" within it a tall, dark and handsome man for every young woman who crossed her palm with silver.

"If we can't talk about business, then why don't you tell me about yourself," Lori said. "After all, I don't have a personnel file."

He smiled at her gentle barb. "I grew up on a farm in a land-locked midwestern state. After high school, I didn't know what I wanted to be, but it wasn't a farmer. I looked for something completely different and worked for a marine salvage company. It was love at first sight with the sea; I absolutely loved it. After a couple years, I knew better what I wanted. I took the money I'd saved and moved to Florida to attend a university with the best marine-related degree program I could find. I got my master's and after working at a communications facility in the Keys, I was offered the directorship here."

"And your parents?"

"They weren't thrilled at my not carrying on the family farm," he admitted, "but they've adjusted. I've never been far from the sea since."

Lori wondered if he missed roaming upon it, remembering the many times she'd seen Joe standing and staring out at the sea—the eternal mistress that forever beckoned—a faraway look on his face.

Jordan was still a fairly young man, in his middle thirties; Joe had been in his late fifties when he'd retired from the merchant marine. "Some men dream of shore when at sea, only to dream of the sea when ashore," Joe had said lightly when Lori once came upon him staring wistfully out at it just before he'd died. Was just being near it enough for Jordan? wondered Lori. He seemed a little restless tonight.

Something she'd read about the shark she'd compared Jordan to earlier came to mind as she watched him look out at the sea through the window overlooking it. In a book he'd co-written with his oceanographer father, Jacques-Yves Cousteau, Philippe Cousteau had written that since sharks didn't possess the kind of anatomy most fish did, they were forced to live in a state of constant movement, swimming unceasingly, day and night, in search not only of food but in order to maintain the vital flow of oxygen through their gills. This magnificent creature they named the splendid savage of the sea was condemned, Philippe wrote, to eternal journeying, to the incessant caress of water against his body, to what he called an implacable, unending love affair with the sea.

Jordan fell silent, toying with the chopsticks on his now empty plate. "Your name fits you," he said after a moment.

"Lori?"

He shook his head. "Lauralee. It has a pretty, soft sound to it, almost like Lorelei. The sea siren."

That's what Joe had said; that was how she'd gotten her nickname. The memory hurt, and she quickly changed the subject, saying lightly, "You're quite safe from me, my singing's so bad—"

"Singing's not the only way to lure a man."

"—that my college roommate begged me not to sing in the shower," she finished, trying not to let him lead her into the subtle duel of words at which he was so adept, into anything that heightened this . . . undercurrent of sexual tension that she'd discerned earlier.

Lori used her chopsticks to lift a piece of ginger from her favorite *furutsu sarada,* the fresh fruit cocktail Mrs. Yamamoto had brought for dessert. She chewed the pungent root meditatively, enjoying the flavor, as Jordan drank his tea.

"You said we'd talk after dinner," she reminded him when she'd finished.

He frowned. "Let's go for a walk. I think my poor legs have gone to sleep."

Lori stood, refusing his hand to help her to her feet, and they left their *o-zashiki.* She studied the back of his dark head as he paid their bill and thanked Mrs. Yamamoto for a meal he told her rivaled the best he'd eaten in Japan.

"So that's how you knew how to use chopsticks," she said as they left the restaurant.

"It was only a couple of meals there on a stopover while I was in the service, but I'm a quick learner," he said with a grin.

They crossed the wooden bridge spanning the dunes to the shore and walked in silence for a time, watching the play of moonlight upon the night-darkened waves.

Finally Lori could bear it no longer. "You're canceling my project, aren't you, Jordan?" she blurted out.

He sighed, stopped to face her. "I'm afraid I'm going to have to temporarily, until I can—"

But unable to listen to another word, Lori cried, "No! Oh, Jordan, no!" Her heart felt as if it were breaking.

"Listen to me, Lori; it's just going to be . . ."

Turning, she ran from him, the wind whispering through the silken folds of her kimono as her feet flew along silently on the hard-packed sand of the shore, uncaring if the sound of her sobs carried back to him.

2

Lori!"

A hand grasped her arm, halting her flight. Pulling ineffectually at the restraint, Lori fiercely blinked back her tears, refusing to turn and look at him. She might be able to stop further tears from falling, but she could do nothing about those that already had, leaving behind trails of moisture in the moonlight like the path left by a sea snail on the sands. "Let me go."

"Only if you let me finish."

"What is there left to say? You said it all," she told him bitterly.

"Lori, turn around and look at me." His voice was soft, but held command. When she did turn, he released her as she'd asked. "I have to cancel the project," he said, "but it'll be *temporary*, Lori."

"Then why does it have to be at all?"

"Because we're just too short of funds. But there *is* a way—"

"What?" she interrupted eagerly.

"A grant. What you've been doing is important, Lori, and I think one of the mental health organizations might fund the project."

"Then how do we go about applying—"

"I've already sent off for a grant application," he interrupted her with a smile.

"Why didn't you tell me?" As soon as the question was out, Lori realized what she'd asked, and knew the answer. "I didn't give you a chance, did I?"

"No, you didn't," he said mildly.

"I'm—sorry."

"It's all right. Why don't we take a walk and talk about it?"

Nodding slowly, she began walking with him along the shore.

"I'm not blind, Lori," Jordan said after a time. "I could see how much you enjoyed working with those kids this afternoon."

"It's more than that. I *enjoy* swimming and I *enjoy* good music." She felt his glance on her at her intensity. "I *need* to help those kids."

"Your shoes are getting wet."

Frowning, Lori looked down and saw that he was right. Stopping, she took them off, trying to ignore the effect of his hand holding her elbow for support as she did. "These kind of shoes don't belong on the beach anyway," she said of the heeled sandals. "I'll go put them up on the dunes so I won't have to carry them." Walking away from him, she used the fact that her back was to him to reach into her clutch purse and extract a pill from the prescription bottle inside. The tension she'd been under was making her ulcer act up. The stretch of beach was empty of other people, so she set her purse down with her shoes, turned and was startled to find Jordan standing behind her with his shoes and socks in hand. Already engaged in the uncomfortable task of trying to swallow the pill dry, Lori choked.

Jordan clapped her on the back. "You okay?"

Lori nodded. "Fine . . . you just surprised me. I didn't hear you come up behind me."

He didn't appear convinced, but when she began walking down to the water's edge, he followed after, tossing his shoes and socks beside her things.

"You were telling me why your work is so important to you."

Lori glanced at him. Two years ago she'd had to do quite a selling job with the former director to get the project started. Not that Ed had been resistant to the idea. You just had to know how to approach him, because if he was in a bad mood, no amount of talking would convince him of a project's worthiness. She barely knew this Jordan Stark, so how could she know what would work best? Should she use facts and figures or appeal to his emotions?

"You don't need to sell me on your project. Just tell me in your own words why it's important to you," he said quietly.

Lori eyed him, a little uncomfortable about how perceptive he was with her. She liked keeping people at arm's length. It was safer that way. Life on land was much like that in the sea—everyone was either predator or prey. Few people could be trusted, really trusted, with your feelings. Better to keep them at a distance, watch them carefully. But she sensed that Jordan wouldn't be satisfied with the explanation she usually gave people. She decided to level with him. She just hoped he wouldn't use what she said against her, say she was being over-emotional. . . .

"These kids are special to me. I don't pity them. Pity means nothing to them, and a lot of people have handicaps even if they're not the kind that show. I'd rather teach one kid who really needs me, who really wants to learn, even if I have to do it over and over, than teach a whole classroom of kids who don't want to, and my kids really want to learn. They try so hard, you saw that. And some of them show so much love—the Down's Syndrome kids especially—it almost hurts *not* to help them in any small way I can. And I've shown that I can help them."

"Is your stomach hurting?"

Lori was thrown off balance by his question. "I— Who says it does?"

He sighed. "Lori, don't play games. I can tell by the way you're rubbing your stomach."

Too absorbed in what she was saying, she hadn't realized she had been. Deliberately she kept her hands at her sides as she walked.

"Is that what you took the pill for?"

"You don't miss much, do you?" she muttered.

"So I've been told. I'm sorry; maybe I shouldn't have asked. I just realized it could be . . . personal."

Even the dim light couldn't conceal the blush rising above his collar. Lori nearly laughed aloud at his embarrassment. "It's not," she said, trying not to smile. "It's no big deal, my stomach just bothers me when I'm upset." Okay, so it was an understatement, but it wasn't a lie, right? she told herself. And besides, her health was none of his business, not her ulcer nor the kind of cramps he'd thought she might be experiencing.

She went on telling him why her work was so important to her, adding that she really thought it was Aphrodite who taught the kids, not her. "I think she loves it even more than I do," she confided, smiling. "She's pretty special; all dolphins are, but she's even more so. Plutarch, the Greek philosopher and biographer, said they don't need us for one single thing and yet dolphins show us nothing but love, love for its own sake, especially for our children. We know how dolphins form sonic images to detect objects in the water, that they can 'hear' the composition and texture of things around them. It's even conceivable that they can use their sonic ability to inspect the contour of internal air spaces, because unlike light, sound travels through flesh and bone and water. But even if that's not true, I think Aphrodite can sense that these kids *need* her, and so she gives them extra love."

"Just like you?"

"I'm not special," she said, shrugging. She studied the waves silvered beneath the moonlight, lifting her kimono skirt a little with one hand to keep it from getting wet in the surf.

"You're such an intriguing contrast, sensitive and vulnerable with those big blue-green eyes of yours, and yet there's a provocativeness about you. . . ."

Lori glanced warily at him, and, as if he sensed her unease and knew he'd overstepped, he went on, "I read once that people who become teachers, doctors, attorneys, are the first children, the eldest in a family. Are you?"

Lori nodded but went no further; there was no need to get into her background when his question had been no more than polite curiosity. "What about you?"

"I was an only child. My parents wanted another one, but somehow it never happened."

"They could have adopted," she blurted out before she could stop herself.

"Yes, they could have," he admitted slowly. "I guess they just kept thinking another would come along, and it was too late before they realized it wouldn't."

There were a lot of those kinds of people, Lori had learned, a lot of people, too, who didn't want to adopt because the child wouldn't be "theirs." She knew it was best not to try to change the minds of the latter. She thought she'd come to terms with the feelings she'd had about the years she'd spent in the orphanage. But Lori found she still had strong feelings about all of it. "At least you had parents," slipped out, and for the second time that night she heard bitterness underlying her words, an emotion she seldom felt.

"Everyone has parents. Biological necessity for our being here." His voice held a trace of humor.

She glanced at him, smiled briefly, then continued to stare straight ahead as she walked. "Of course. I didn't mean to sound the way I did. It's just a shame that people like your parents couldn't have adopted a child before they felt it was too late to do it, that's all. About the grant . . ."

"You really have a one-track mind," he said with a smile. Then he was growing serious. "Or is it that I was getting too close again?"

"You said you wanted to meet with me about the project," she pointed out.

"Yes, I said that, didn't I?"

He was silent for a moment, studying her with an intentness that was unnerving, and she wished she could tell what he was thinking. He hadn't touched her, yet his words about her had been like a caress to her senses, as tangible as the warm water lapping at her bare ankles and the soft breeze blowing against her face. Immersed as she'd been with her college and graduate studies, with her work at the facility, Lori had seldom dated and felt out of her depth with a man like Jordan, so attractive and self-assured, a man who could stalk a woman as a shark would his prey. Dinner in the intimate *o-zashiki,* this stroll in the moonlight by the sea, were supposed to be for the purpose of talking about her work, not of setting the stage for something personal. "When do you think we'll hear about the grant?"

"I don't know. These things take time."

"Time, time," she muttered. "What if I lose all the progress I've made with the kids?" Then something even worse came to mind. What if they didn't get the grant at all? She voiced her concern to Jordan, who told her not to go worrying about that before it happened. "I can't help it," Lori responded, biting her bottom lip.

"Worry can give you an ulcer," Jordan told her. He

glanced sharply at her, and she wondered if it was because it had suddenly occurred to him why she'd taken the pill earlier. "Don't do it, Lori. Let me worry about it for now." He reached out and touched her lips with one finger, stroking the bottom one, and she heard her own indrawn breath at the sudden, unexpected caress. "And stop biting these. I can think of much nicer things to do with them."

His eyes held her spellbound; she felt herself drawn into their fathomless black depths. The sound of the restless sea began fading, fading. Then his shoulder blocked out the light of the moon behind him as he stepped toward her. A strange breathlessness washed over her, and she was powerless to move, as if the sand beneath her feet had turned to shifting quicksand.

He was going to kiss her; she sensed it even before his face drew nearer and his mouth hovered close to her own. A wave splashed at her ankle, higher than it had been, as the tide came inexorably in toward shore. Brought back to reality, she used the water wetting the hem of her kimono as an excuse to step to one side. She began walking again, aware of his puzzled eyes on her as he joined her. Effortlessly, as if there had been nothing but a break in it, he picked up their conversation about the project. They discussed other places to apply for grants, should the one Jordan had applied to not come through with funding, and then talked about plans he had for the facility. The moment that had seemed to stretch for an eternity between them vanished, as if carried out to sea by the tide. She became less and less nervous of him, as he made no attempt to touch her or kiss her again, until finally she told herself she must have imagined that his moving toward her had any significance.

The breeze off the sea turned cool, riffling the fronds of the palm trees that lined the beach so that they resembled huge black sea anemones out of water. Jordan suggested that they turn to walk back in the direction from which they'd come. Lori was surprised to see how far they'd wandered, and found herself wishing she'd brought a wrap. Her kimono had been warm enough without a wrap earlier this evening, but now she felt the need of one.

Jordan must have seen her shiver, for he was taking off his jacket and draping it around her shoulders despite her protests that he'd be cold. When he insisted, she subsided, grateful for the warmth, although with it came the tantalizing scent of his aftershave, which she'd been too aware of during dinner, when they'd sat so close.

They slipped on their shoes and walked to Jordan's car in the restaurant parking lot. He drove her to her apartment nearby; she lived so close she'd walked over. At her door, she waited for the inevitable request to come inside that dates always made. Even though this hadn't been a date, things had gotten a little personal as they talked, and she knew by those words about her supposed "provocativeness" that he was attracted to her. She remembered all too well that he'd seemed about to kiss her before she'd moved away.

But Jordan didn't ask to come inside; he didn't turn into the octopus most of those dates became. He took his jacket from her and slipped it on. When the cool breeze touched her again and she shivered slightly, he slid his hands up and down her arms beneath the wide sleeves of the kimono, warming her. "You'd better get inside," he said.

She hadn't wanted to have to wrestle him off, to create bad feelings between them, especially when they had to work together. So why, she asked herself, was she left with such a lingering disappointment when Jordan . . . merely left?

"That's it," Betsy crooned her approval, taking each of Timmy's arms, gently helping them to carve an arc one at a time, as she swam on her back, the child atop her tummy. "Just like Aphrodite, Timmy; we're really swimming the backstroke with our fins, huh?"

Betsy was helping Timmy with one of the exercises taught her and Lori by the physical therapist on staff at the local Special Children's Center. Lori sat at the side of the tank, watching them, as she dangled her legs in the water. Usually she really enjoyed this part of the classes, seeing how the children took such delight in mimicking the movements of Aphrodite in the water with Betsy's support. Physical exercise was as important to the children as mental "stretching," only with Aphrodite's help, the exercises, just like the lessons, were just pure fun for them.

Timmy laughed, and the sound echoed around the tank. But instead of making Lori smile, as the laughter of one of her kids always did, today the scene before her made her feel sad. How many more lessons and sessions in physical therapy would she and Betsy be able to give before Jordan transferred them to other work?

"And here's Lori Long-face!" Betsy cried as she and Timmy approached Lori. "Say 'Hi, Lori Long-face,' Timmy!"

He did so cheerfully, his face splitting in a grin, and Lori had to smile.

Betsy did another lap around the pool with the tireless Aphrodite and the equally tireless Timmy, then handed him to his parent. She swam over to Lori. "Hey, cheer up, kid!" she chided, slicking her bright red hair back from her face and then leaning her arms on the concrete edge of the tank beside Lori. "Things aren't as bad as you're making them look."

"You're taking the news well," Lori said with a sigh. "I wish I could be like you sometimes."

"Only sometimes?" asked Betsy irreverently, laughing when Lori said, "Oh, *you!*"

Aphrodite leaped from the water, a silvery flash of spinning body before she dove back into the depths of the tank.

"You know what I mean. You're a lot like Aphrodite, so free-spirited about everything."

"Lori, life's too short to brood about things," Betsy told her, climbing up the metal steps from the tank to dry her hair and body with a towel. Like Lori, she wore a quite modest one-piece navy swimsuit. The suit was even the same size as Lori's. But on Betsy, well, how the suit accommodated her generous proportions was surely a testament to the stretchability of nylon, Lori couldn't help thinking. Quite a few of the men at the facility found excuses to stop by— supposedly to watch the progress of the lessons—until Lori had to post a memo on the bulletin board asking others to stay away.

"We'll get the grant; you'll see," said Betsy calmly, just as she had twice that morning.

Lori wished she could take things the way Betsy did. She lacked the optimism of her friend and co-worker. She lacked her ability to bounce back from a romance gone wrong, too. In the four years she'd known her, Betsy had been dumped by boyfriends three times, and she'd stopped seeing others about whom she'd been serious. Yet she'd never been devastated by the experiences, never "brooded," as Betsy had said a moment ago. And Lori still occasionally thought about how the one serious relationship she'd had with a man—one who used to work here—had gone. Betsy never let an experience with a man make her view them with wariness, as Lori had after breaking off with Robert. "There's other fish in the sea, honey; you shouldn't let one keep you from dropping in the bait and hooking another who might be lots better for you," was the way Betsy had put it.

"Besides," Betsy was saying, fastening her wrapa-round skirt, "you let this thing get you down, the grant, I mean, and you just let it spoil one more day that it shouldn't. Now, are we going for lunch or not? As I remember, it's your turn to treat, but if you promise to stop with that Emmett Kelly face, I'll spring for The Salad Barge."

Smiling at Betsy's comparing her face to that of the sad circus clown, Lori put on a smile, and they went to lunch.

A day later they were transferred from the teaching project, which was suspended.

"Just like that," Lori said numbly, reading the

request from Jordan that she and Betsy report to their new assignments.

"Think 'temporary,'" said Betsy bracingly. Only later did Lori realize that Betsy had kept asking for her help with therapy sessions that afternoon so that she wouldn't have a chance to think about the transfer.

Lori's new co-worker was the complete opposite of Betsy. Chad Bennett was studious and balding—although they were about the same age. He chewed his nails from nervousness and had a habit of running his hands through his sparse hair, making it look rather like a pile of limp brown seaweed. Chad had been content to work without help in his current project. The transfer of Lori into his crowded little office had him even more upset than she—if that were possible, she thought. She was forced to smile a little at the way he moved jerkily around his office, apologizing like some absentminded professor for the lack of a space to sit as he moved a pile of computer disks, papers and professional journals from one place only to set them down in the same place a few seconds later.

That was her last smile. The work that Chad did was totally different from her one-on-one work with the kids and Aphrodite. Chad sat before a computer screen keyboarding equations so abstruse Lori wondered if he were using another language, and not just computerese, either. He explained that what he was doing was setting up a code of sounds that would allow man and dolphins to communicate. All the while he was explaining his work in animated tones, Lori was wishing she'd just been allowed to go on communicating in her own way with her own dolphin.

Left with a word processor she'd had little previous

experience using, confined indoors with what basically amounted to a secretarial position, Lori longed to be outside doing her work—which had always been more play than work, more love than science studied for science's sake.

By the end of the week Chad had acclimated himself to Lori's presence in his sanctum, but she had been driven insane—quietly, of course; her occasional exclamation of dismay over her efforts at the processor had Chad starting in surprise.

"At least think about my idea," she begged Betsy over lunch. "Even if the kids aren't missing the lessons—I am!"

"But if Jordan found out—"

"He won't find out. I have a key to the gate at our area, and we'll do it after everybody's gone. Betsy, *please?*" she wheedled.

Betsy hesitated, plainly torn.

"I'm sure it'll only be for a few days, just until the grant goes through. You said yourself it would."

"Oh, Lori, that's low," Betsy said, groaning. "Using my own words against me!"

In the end Betsy gave in, as Lori had known she would. Betsy had a soft heart for the children, too, and enjoyed what she did.

Some of the parents weren't as easy to convince. "Lori, we don't want you and Betsy to lose your jobs," several said, shaking their heads uncertainly when Lori assured them that wouldn't happen. But in the end they, too, had to give in to her argument and their children's repeated requests.

A week later there had still been no word about the

grant. Lori went to eat a packed lunch beside Aphrodite's tank during the midday break, but it sat, untouched, while she trailed her bare legs in the water. There was a grayness to the day that would have been depressing even if there weren't a reason for the way Lori felt now. Dipping her toes idly into the water, she scanned the leaden clouds overhead. They were full of rain that had threatened to fall all day. Even the water in Aphrodite's tank had a grayish cast beneath the sunless sky instead of its usual aquamarine tint.

A pointed silver nose nudged at Lori's hand. She patted it absently, then watched as Aphrodite sped toward the other end of the tank. The dolphin's body cleaved backward through the water, and she made other bids for Lori's attention. Then she returned to where Lori sat, prodding Lori's hand with her nose, merry invitation on her seraphic, seemingly perpetually smiling face.

"No, Aphrodite, I don't want to play," she told the dolphin with a sigh, shaking her head. She thought about putting the wraparound skirt she'd worn over a matching ice-green leotard back on. Many of the women on staff at the facility dressed as she did; it was more convenient when working in and around the water as they did here. Lori had discarded the skirt, intending to swim for a while with Aphrodite and then eat her lunch before heading back to work. But so far she'd done neither.

The night she and Jordan had walked the beach and talked about her project she'd told him how sensitive dolphins were about each other's mental and physical conditions, and Aphrodite to the children's.

Now Aphrodite used the rich variety of sounds she could make, and Lori didn't need Chad's or anyone else's code to know the dolphin was trying to comfort her. Aphrodite swam over to her and thrust the upper portion of her body into Lori's lap. She flapped her fins, chattering in a soft, mournful manner, her dark eyes seemed to stare sorrowfully into Lori's.

The dolphin's instinctive effort to console her reminded Lori of the first dolphin to do so, the one she'd met at Aqua World—Joe's and Polly's marine park—years ago. Depressed, she stroked Aphrodite's shiny head and felt a tear slide down her cheek. Her work was the most important thing in her life, and now she didn't have even that. . . .

"But mermaids have no tears."

Lori jerked her head up, startled, and saw Jordan striding toward her with that lithe, animal sort of grace of his, his footsteps silent on the concrete.

She stared at him, surprised. It wasn't just that she hadn't expected him here. Who would have thought he'd read Hans Christian Andersen's "The Little Mermaid" as a boy, let alone remembered a line from it as an adult?

Before she could say anything, he was telling her, "I must say, those legs were worth the price of a voice, however sweet."

Recalling how in the story the mermaid had traded her voice for legs so that she could join the man she loved on land, and seeing him gazing at hers appreciatively, she said quickly, "I—you startled me, that's all." A thought occurred to her, and she looked up eagerly. "Did you hear about the grant?"

"Hello, Jordan," he said. "Nice to see you."

Lori blushed as she realized she'd been rude. "I'm sorry. Hello, Jordan. It *is* nice to see you." Well, almost, she thought.

"You've been avoiding me."

"I haven't," she protested. Another lie. . . .

"Yes, you have," he disagreed equably.

Lori shifted a little uneasily as Jordan lowered himself to sit beside her on the ledge of the tank, so close their bare thighs touched. He wore one of the white short-sleeved sport shirts printed with the aqua and sea-blue wave logo of the facility both men and women here were given for their use. A pair of many-pocketed white denim shorts revealed thighs and long legs that, like his arms, were bronzed and well-muscled, covered with dark, curling hair.

Aphrodite acknowledged Jordan cheerfully but stayed as she was, head and upper body lying on Lori's lap.

His lips twisted in a wry grin, Jordan asked, "Don't tell me she's going to avoid me too? Aphrodite, I swear, Scout's honor"—he held up his hand—"I'm doing everything I can to get the grant for her going again. I know Lori's upset, but I wouldn't do anything to hurt her for the world. You know that, don't you?"

She stared at him for a long moment with those knowing, so expressive eyes of hers; then she looked again at Lori. Impulsively Lori bent and kissed Aphrodite's head. "I'm okay, really, girl." Glancing up, Lori caught the expression of . . . envy? on Jordan's face. Then, becoming aware of her eyes on him, it vanished. Knowing how intuitive he'd been of what she'd thought the night they'd had dinner and walked the beach, she straightened and carefully made her own face politely blank. "Anyway, I wasn't crying."

"Maybe not, but you certainly look down."

Aphrodite slipped from Lori's lap and went to play with a ball that floated on the water in the center of the tank, as if to say that now Jordan was here to talk with Lori, she'd be all right. Lori used the dolphin's playful activity as an excuse not to look at Jordan, but she knew he watched her. After a moment she picked up the sandwich at her side and, folding the foil around it so that Jordan couldn't see that she hadn't eaten it, shoved it back into the paper sack. "I've got to get back."

"That's funny; Chad said you'd just come up here."

Lori bit her lip, said, "Yes, well, I've finished lunch, so I might as well get back to work."

Naturally her stomach had to pick that moment to growl and give proof to her lie.

"Must have been seafoam," he said dryly. He'd heard her protesting stomach. "At least, I think that's what mermaids eat."

A little shamefaced, she said, "Periwinkle soup, actually."

At his upraised eyebrows, she explained, "I worked at a marine park after school and full-time during summer vacation, did a little of everything from taking tickets to feeding the dolphins to looking for lost children. One of my jobs was to play mermaid in a tail of emerald and sapphire sequins that covered my legs and two shells that covered—er, my top." Her blush deepened, and she hurried on. "I was supposed to swim in this glass tank and lead the crowd from the seal show to the dolphin show, as a sort of a watery Pied Piper. Sometimes I'd entertain the kids with stories about the mermaid."

"So was periwinkle soup the only thing you were supposed to eat? Doesn't sound much more substantial than seafoam."

She laughed. "No, let me see, there was sea cucumber salad and thousand island dressing. Sponge cake for dessert, of course. Oh, and peanut butter and—"

"Let me guess: peanut butter and jellyfish sandwiches!" Jordan finished with a laugh.

Lori pretended astonishment. "I didn't see you in the audience." She smiled. "It was a lot of fun."

"Is that all there was to your story?"

Laughing, she told him he was as bad as the children who always wanted to hear "more, more!" "I ended up with quite a story by the time I got through answering all their questions. No, as I remember it, the people at Aqua World caught the mermaid when she followed a dolphin there, a very special dolphin she talked with when they swam in the sea together, one that answered her just like another person. Not in people talk, but they always understood each other. The mermaid was very lonely because she had no parents, you see, just this friendly wrinkled old walrus who kept an eye on her when no one else wanted her. He made sure she ate and brushed her teeth—flossing them with strands of seaweed, of course!—and wrote her lessons in the sand with a sea-pen. And at night he tucked her into her bed, a big hollow shell on the bottom of the sea. But one morning he wasn't there anymore, and so the mermaid and the dolphin went looking for him. They got caught in a fisherman's net, and that's how they came to be at Aqua World."

She paused for a breath and went on. "The mermaid wasn't happy at Aqua World at first. But there was a man who loved her like the old walrus. He even looked a little like him—you know, the same big bristly mustache and floppy cheeks. I'd puff out my cheeks like this and nod my head. There wasn't much more to the story, just that the man would tuck her in every night and tell her stories about the sea and make her feel less lonely. She had other friends, too, besides her dolphin friend, lots of nice fish and bird and animal and people friends. The kids would always ask if they lived happily ever after, of course."

"Did they?"

"Yes, they did," she said after a moment. "The kind man went away one day, just as the old walrus had. The mermaid and the dolphin missed him, but they knew it was time for them to take care of themselves."

"No prince? I thought—"

"Different story," Lori said a little tersely, realizing that she'd been so caught up in the story that she hadn't realized Jordan had evidently thought more of it was the truth than it was. Not the part about being a mermaid, of course, but the part about the loneliness and Joe. "Not that unrequited love and tears as in 'Little Mermaid' aren't the usual result of a woman becoming involved with a man."

"Fairy tales are like life," Jordan spoke softly. "They are—*it is*—what you make of it."

"Yes, well, it was just a story I made up for the kids. It wasn't about me."

"No?"

Lori glanced at him sharply. "I wasn't crying," she told him with a trace of defensiveness. "I'd just been petting Aphrodite and I must have gotten water on my cheek, that's all."

"I wish you'd let me get as close to you as you do Aphrodite." His hand touched her cheek as she glanced away, not wanting to trust the tenderness she saw in his eyes. Sensing her reserve, he told her, "Eat your lunch; don't let my being here keep you from it. And don't say you aren't hungry; I heard your stomach, remember?"

"I'm really not—"

"Eat!" he ordered. Then, his expression softening, he added, "Please." He turned and called, "Hey, Aphrodite, you come tell her. Even when I said *please* she wouldn't eat her lunch."

Aphrodite swam over to nod and add her encouragement, levering up out of the water enough to grasp Lori's almost waist-length braid and tweak it gently, like a mischievous child might.

Lori laughed. "All right, all right, I'll eat!" She glanced at Jordan. "That is, if you'll join me. I brought enough for two because Betsy was going to have lunch with me, only she had a better offer."

"Better than this?" With his hand Jordan gestured at the sun that was finally breaking through the clouds to cast its golden glow down at them, at the water that sparkled aquamarine in the tank, at the lunch she placed between them.

"Well, it was more *who* she was going to be with than where she'd be eating and what she'd be eating, you see."

"I see," he said with a grin. "Actually, I don't. I can't

47

imagine being in any better company, but then, I guess it's not the same for Betsy as it is for me, hmm?''

Part of her expanded inside at his words, part of her watched as if from outside her and said, My, doesn't he have a smooth line! She merely smiled and handed him his sandwich, then bit into hers. She caught him looking dubiously at the vegetable that topped the pita bread filled with cubes of cheese and chopped lettuce and tomatoes in an oil and vinegar dressing. ''That's not seaweed, in case you're wondering. It's alfalfa sprouts.''

''I know.'' He took a bite. ''Say, this isn't half bad, although it could use a little meat in it. Are you a health-food nut?''

Lori poured iced tea from a Thermos into paper cups. ''You sound like Betsy. She calls it a salad in a roll and always wants to know if I've brought along a hamburger so it's a *real* meal. No, I'm not a health-food nut, I just prefer food like this, although, given the choice, I would rather eat fish than red meat, with all the chemicals cattle are fed.''

At the mention of fish, Aphrodite joined them, her ball forgotten. Lori and Jordan laughed as she looked hopefully for a handout.

''It's a wonder you don't get fat, as much as you eat,'' he told the dolphin.

Aphrodite dipped beneath the water and emerged, sending water spraying through her blowhole. A few drops landed on Jordan's legs, sparkling like diamonds when caught in his dark, curling hair.

''She did that on porpoise,'' he accused.

''Oh, Aphrodite, did you hear that awful joke?'' Lori

gasped, pretending to swoon, secretly liking the way he wasn't above such a joke. The dolphin obligingly rolled over in the water until Jordan shouted with laughter.

"The two of you are against me," he told them, shaking his head. He looked seriously at Lori. "You even look a lot alike."

Lori grimaced. "You mean the way people tend to look like their dogs?" An image came to mind of a man she knew who owned a basset hound; the man's face was as long and sad and jowly as his pet's. "How?"

"See her smile? There are those who think a dolphin's smile is just physiology. But I for one don't think it's just that. I think their faces really reflect their nature—kind, intelligent, loving. As for you, how you resemble her . . . it's more a similarity of expression than a physical one. Even when you're not smiling, your lips curve upward just a little, more when you're happy, less when you're sad, but always there's a bit of an inner smile showing through. And I see a resemblance in your eyes, too, large, expressive, trusting. Well, not always as trusting when you look at me." There was a note of regret in his voice she couldn't miss. "Why don't you trust me, Lori?"

Lori rewrapped the brownie left after the one she'd eaten and the two Jordan consumed. "I can't imagine why you think I don't trust you," she prevaricated, paying great attention to what she was doing.

"You're sure it's not because I had to suspend your project temporarily?"

"Positive," she asserted, even though she knew that wasn't true.

"And you won't avoid me anymore?"

She started to repeat that she hadn't, but couldn't do it honestly. Under his level stare she found herself admitting, "That wouldn't be fair."

"Then there's no reason why we can't go out again."

Caught by surprise, she was about to remind him that they hadn't gone out before, that it had been business. But he was taking her assent for granted, saying, "Good, I'll pick you up at seven."

"Wait a minute, not tonight! I . . . that is, I have something I have to do." She didn't, but she had to get used to the idea of going out with this man first.

"Oh? If it's something like washing your hair, just say so."

"Why? Am I not supposed to need to do that?"

"It's just that it's been my experience that when someone finds reasons why they can't do something and they're not very good reasons, it's usually that they didn't really want to do whatever it was in the first place."

How could you fault logic like that? Part of her wanted to be with him. She'd been attracted to him that night at dinner, even before; she'd found herself talking with him as she couldn't remember doing with a man other than Joe. Yet part of her was afraid of her attraction for him. And Lori was not used to being afraid of anything. The way she usually dealt with a fear was to confront it head-on. "I suppose I could do it some other night." She watched his slow smile, and it stirred conflicting emotions of anticipation and yet unease at the same time.

"See you later then." He got to his feet, started to walk away, then turned to look over his shoulder. "Thanks for lunch."

"My pleasure," she said, and as she spoke, she realized it really had been.

3

Jordan showed up at her door dressed in a casual white open-necked shirt, tan slacks and a natural-colored linen jacket, so her choice of a simple blue cotton pique sun dress and shawl of the same material in case the night grew cool was a good one.

Expecting to be taken to a restaurant, Lori was surprised when Jordan drove to the marina. There they boarded a large steamer-type boat, *The Florida Queen*, that had once been used for cruises up and down the Intracoastal Waterway. He led Lori to an area on deck where tables were arranged around a small stage and seated her with the air of a man who had been there before. "I'll be right back," he said, then left her.

He returned with a thin young man with a curling mass of blond hair and a wide grin who carried three wineglasses and a bottle of champagne. "Hello, Lori, good to see you."

"Darryl, I haven't seen you for weeks! How's the job with Baxters' coming?"

He uncorked the bottle and poured the champagne into the glasses he'd set on the table. "I'm working here now."

Several men, obviously members of a small band, were setting up instruments on the small stage.

"Oh? Is someone going to start taking *The Queen* for cruises again?"

"Yes," said Darryl, grinning even wider. "Me." He lifted his glass and turned to Jordan, started to say something, but was interrupted by Jordan's proposing a toast to the success of his venture.

"Which wouldn't have been possible without you," Darryl inserted.

"Oh?" Lori looked curiously at Jordan.

"Isn't it time to cast off? And how do you get service around here, anyway?"

Darryl just chuckled, not taking offense. "Modesty prevents his telling you, Lori, but I'll tell you. Jordan here talked the bank into making the loan for me to buy *The Queen*." He lifted his glass in toast, saying, "To you, friend."

"That was nice of you, Jordan," Lori said quietly after Darryl had gone.

"Anyone would have done it," he muttered, still glaring after Darryl, who was sauntering down the passage to the cabin. "The two of you act as if I loaned him the money myself."

"Instead of just cosigning the loan?"

His head jerked up. "How'd you know . . .?" Then he realized her question had been a guess. Shrugging, he told her, "He's good for it. He's just had some tough breaks lately."

Lori studied Jordan, seeing a new side of him. The engines rumbled, and the boat eased away from shore. "Hey, isn't he going to wait for more passengers?"

"Darryl told me he wanted to take the boat out for a shake-down run," Jordan informed her, pouring them both more wine. "The cruises begin tomorrow night."

The Florida Queen moved slowly down the waterway, and the band began to play. Lori sat back in her chair, enjoying the soft breeze that lifted her hair from her neck. The music was equally soft, producing its own restful effect as dusk fell and lights began flickering on along the shore. Stars came out, reflected in the midnight-dark waters surrounding the pleasure boat.

"Like it?" Jordan asked her.

"Love it."

They talked about *The Queen*'s past, and as they admired her freshly painted and refurbished appearance, Jordan told Lori about Darryl's plans for *The Queen*'s future. A "sight-seeing and tanning" cruise was set for several afternoons a week, dinner cruises each evening and moonlight party cruises from nine to midnight. Darryl hoped a cruise featuring music from the big band era one night a week would attract the substantial older population.

Their conversation about the boat they were on led Jordan to tell Lori a story about his work in marine salvage. He glossed over the danger she knew such

work entailed, emphasizing the rewards he'd found in
a job where men learned to depend on each other for
their very survival beneath a sea that could embrace
them like a lover or draw them to their death.

His talking about the salvage business turned her
thoughts to *The Queen* and his role in making her new
life possible. In a small town like this, everyone knew
everyone else's business, and it was no secret that
Darryl had had a hard time lately. He and his wife had
both worked long hours to save money to start a
restaurant, and then their infant daughter's illness had
wiped them out financially. How kind of Jordan to
come to the rescue, thought Lori. She couldn't help
hoping he'd be able to work the same magic with the
grant papers for her project. As she did, she remembered what he'd said earlier that day: "I'd give her the
money myself if I could," he'd told Aphrodite. But he
couldn't do that—not that she'd expected it.

"You're quiet."

She smiled at him, not wanting to tell him what
she'd been thinking about and maybe spoil the mood.
"This is just perfect," she told him, lifting her hand to
encompass the boat and the music. The breeze, warm
but still pleasant, riffled through their hair and rippled
the water so that the reflections of the stars upon it
turned to shattered diamonds of light.

Darryl's wife, Fran, served a seafood sampler and
chatted for a moment before leaving them to enjoy
their meal. After they'd eaten, as Lori walked with
Jordan around *The Queen*, she caught a glimpse of
Darryl and Fran celebrating with champagne in the
galley. Jordan had taken Lori's hand to help her up

some stairs and then continued to hold it. Lori squeezed his to alert him to the scene. "See what you helped make possible?" she whispered.

"They didn't need anyone to make *that* possible," he whispered back with a smile as the two, oblivious to witnesses, embraced happily. "Two people who truly love each other don't need anything from anybody. They've got it all." He glanced at her. "Love's no fairy tale, Lori."

His words reminded her of her own that afternoon. "No?"

"No," he said in a firm voice.

They tiptoed away. "Let's dance," he said when they returned to their table, leading her out onto the dance area before the stage.

In his arms, Lori forgot that they were the only couple there. She became totally immersed in the feel of his arms, strong and hard around her. The scent of the tangy aftershave that clung to his skin, the movement of his body against her own as they danced, were all that existed for her.

His thighs touched hers through the thin cotton dress she wore. Hands crossed behind her back, Jordan stroked her hair, holding her close as they swayed to the music. Dancing brought Jordan closer than they'd ever been; there was an excitement in just dancing with him she hadn't felt with other men, adding to the attraction that drew her to him.

"I've finally got you where I want you," he murmured, his mouth close to her ear. "You can't run away from me here."

She pulled away from him a little and looked up at him. "Are you going to do something to make me want to run?" she asked, trying to sound light. His touch was entirely too disturbing. . . .

He smiled, his teeth a gleam of white against tanned skin. Am I going to *do* something or do I *want* to do something?" His warm breath fanned her cheeks as he spoke.

"What—whatever." She stammered a little, too conscious of his warm breath on her lips as he lowered his head. "What are you doing?"

"The better to hear you, my dear. My, what big eyes you have." His eyes gleamed with mischief.

"So you read 'Little Red Riding Hood' as well as 'The Little Mermaid,' huh?"

"I was a kid once too, you know, and little boys read fairy tales just like little girls do."

"I'll just bet the wolf was your favorite character."

"Now, why do you say that?" he asked, humor still lacing his deep voice. "Are you afraid I want to gobble you up?" When she didn't answer him, he gathered her close again, and feeling a strange rumbling in his chest, she came to realize he was shaking with silent laughter.

"I'm not going to gobble you up, Lori. I'm just going to wear you down like the tide does a rock—until you have no resistance to me left."

If he knew how little I have to begin with, thought Lori, adrift in his arms.

Jordan had told her Darryl planned to have the music on the cruises suited to the differing tastes of those who took them. Tonight the music was for lovers, the tempo slow and seductive and suited for slow, close dancing, and if the thought briefly surfaced that the selections had been planned just for them, she quickly forgot it again. One song followed another and still they danced as the boat glided through the peaceful river beneath a glowing moon.

When she realized the band had quit playing and they'd been dancing to their own private music, Lori drew back a little in his arms, glancing up with an embarrassed smile at Jordan. He was staring down at her, and the emotion she read in his dark, intense eyes—a desire for her deeper than any she'd ever glimpsed in a man's eyes—threw her own emotions into turmoil. "I think we're about to dock," she tried to say lightly, but she noted the gleam in his eyes and the smile that touched the corners of the mouth so close to hers, and she knew he must have sensed something of what she felt.

His head lowered, blocking out the moonlight, and his mouth brushed hers. Lori backed away from the intimacy of his kiss, too aware of the musicians packing away their instruments. He let her go and walked with her to the rail to watch as they approached the shore.

On the way home he put the top down on the car, and they drove along the long, quiet stretch of ocean highway. They discussed the certainty that the dinner and party cruises Darryl planned would be a success. Jordan predicted that a crowd of at least a hundred would show up the next night on the inaugural cruise.

"Two hundred," said Lori.

"I don't think they can seat that many."

"Then people will have to stand, because with the kind of food they served, there won't be two hundred, there'll be three hundred," Lori told him, increasing her original estimate.

"I can see *The Queen* sinking into the river right now," he said, glancing over to grin at her.

"If we didn't sink her after all the food we ate, it'll never sink."

"Just because you ate enough oysters Rockefeller to bankrupt a millionaire. . . ." He'd teased her about going into raptures over the appetizer. "I just wish Darryl would have let me pay; he's going to need every cent for a long time before he's in the clear. And I don't just mean with his business."

"Often when people are least able to make a gesture is the time they really need to make it. He needed to show you how much what you'd done meant to him."

"I guess you're right." He appeared somewhat unconvinced.

"Look, if it bothers you that much, maybe you could find some other way to make him take the money?"

"Like how?"

"I don't know; I'd have to think about it for a minute. I'm not good at being devious at a moment's notice." Her conscience pricked at that. Giving lessons behind his back could be labeled devious. She wondered what he'd do if he found out. Maybe if she told him now, while they were out and he was in a good mood . . .

Then he was saying he could almost hear the whirring in her mind, so had she come up with anything?

Caught unprepared, she fumbled around for something to say and blurted out the first thing that came to mind: "Since we liked the dinner and cruise so much, maybe we can recommend it to others." At his glance, which seemed to ask if that was the best she could do, she thought harder. "What about having the office party there on the boat next month?"

"That's better."

"Well, I did tell you I wasn't good being devious at a moment's notice."

"I shudder to think how you'd be with time to plan."

She shot him a quick glance. What would he think if he knew that she was carrying on with the project behind his back? He must have seen her shiver because he asked, "Are you warm enough? I can put the top up."

"I'm fine. Besides, it's too pretty a night to do that."

Keeping one hand on the wheel, he reached over with the other and gathered her close to him, tucking the shawl around her. Far from being soothing, the touch of his hand was disturbing, and Lori forced her attention on the view. They passed the small city zoo as they drove to her apartment, and her breath caught in delight at the sight of two white swans gliding on the mirrorlike surface of a small pond edged with willows.

"Want me to stop?"

At her nod, Jordan pulled the car off the road and they got out and walked down to the edge of the pond. Silently they watched the water courtship of the swans, who were rubbing their long, graceful necks together. The scene was poignantly beautiful, more so because Lori knew that swans were said to mate for life. She wished Jordan wouldn't stand so close; tonight she felt so vulnerable to him.

His hand touched the side of her neck, stroking the long bare length of it, pushing aside the silky fall of hair from her shoulder to better trace the line from her earlobe to the hollow of her throat, where her pulse beat madly.

She moved away from his hand. "Have you been here before?"

"No, not yet. Why?"

"It's a nice little zoo for a town that isn't very big."

"That's nice, Lori. I'll remember that."

Ignoring the dryness in his tone, she said, "Come here and I'll show you my second favorite animals." One of the things Lori liked best about the zoo was that it was designed so that it was never locked. "They have a pair of otters here that are darling." Swiftly she walked toward the area where they were enclosed. Rounding a corner, she was plunged into total darkness. The lights on this side of the zoo were out for some reason, she realized. For a moment she stood there in the dark, trying to get her bearings. She heard no footsteps, yet became aware of another presence —Jordan? She waited for him to speak or touch her, and when the moments stretched and still there was no sign of him she began to wonder if he'd left her here. She wouldn't exactly blame him—what grown man out on a date wanted to go wandering around a zoo? Much as she loved animals, she hadn't wanted to go looking at them tonight either. But she'd grown nervous of his nearness, afraid he was going to touch her again, to try to kiss her. And she wasn't ready for that yet, not with him.

She waited in the darkness, unafraid, just as she was

in the sea. After all, she told herself, she could just retrace her steps and she'd be back in the light again. The dark only contained what was there in the light.

But Jordan was there in the light, in the daytime, and she sensed him now in the dark. "Jordan?"

"I was wondering if you'd ever get nervous and call out," he drawled close by. She jumped in spite of herself and was grateful for the concealing cloak of night. "You could have said something, not stood there so quiet. I'm not interested in playing games, Jordan."

"No? Then why don't you stop playing them with me?"

"I'm not!" She started walking in the direction she'd come and bumped into something solid. She backed away, but his hands grasped her arms and held her.

"Don't go." Jordan's words came in a whisper, but they were sharp and clear in the silence of the night. "Don't run from me, Lori, from what we've been sensing about each other from that first day on the beach."

He held her, but he didn't try to restrain her or draw her closer. His voice was low, coaxing, as if he knew that using greater physical or psychological persuasion would only frighten her away. He stood so close, she could breathe in the special scent that she recognized as part aftershave, part clean male fragrance. His heart beat rapidly beneath her hands, and she could hear the slow inhalation and exhalation of his breath. The feel of him holding her, even if just by the arms, of their standing together in darkness, was sensual, intimate.

His hands brought her closer. "I've wanted to kiss you all night," he said, very close now.

She discovered she wanted that too, wanted to feel his mouth on her lips, wanted to feel them moving against hers. Rising up on her toes, she searched for his mouth, unerringly found it and tentatively touched her slightly parted lips to his. A taste, she told herself, and that would be enough. Just a kiss, and she'd stop; and he'd let her, she could tell that from his manner. . . .

But when she felt his mouth move beneath hers, supple and persuasive, seeming to give new shape and texture to her own in the process, she discovered she couldn't stop; she didn't want to stop.

His tongue glided between her lips to touch hers, and a low roaring began to fill her ears, a sound like the one you heard when you held a shell to your ear. The sound intensified the strange, unreal quality of their being totally enclosed, not just against all intrusion from sight, but from any world but their own. Their hands, trapped between them, only heightened the effect of their erotic intimacy.

Kissing him, she felt like an inexperienced swimmer thrown into the deep end of the pool. Kissing him was thrilling, overwhelming. Her arms went up around his neck, and she leaned against him as her knees trembled and threatened to buckle.

The filmy folds of her skirt moved in the breeze like fronds of seaweed drifting in the currents of the sea, wrapping intimately between and around his legs. Their kiss deepened, became more compelling, and Jordan's arms stole around her to bring her closer and closer. Instead of supporting her, his touch only served to weaken her all the more. His hands moved over her back, caressing her bare skin above the scooped back of the dress and the hair and the material covering the rest of her back. She was swept deeper and deeper into a spinning dark vortex with him, wanting him to take her with him down into its depths and into her own innermost being . . .

She felt one of his hands move from behind her back to slide over a breast, cupping its braless softness, his thumb rubbing gently over its center until he felt the nipple harden in response. He caught her moan in his mouth and kissed her again, his other hand sliding down to cup the curve of hip and buttock, to bring her even closer to his desire, which pressed hard against her.

"God, how I want to make love to you, Lori," he whispered against her lips. "You feel so damned good to me."

Imagining herself making love to him, the black velvet canvas of the night as background, was easy. She saw them lying naked in each other's arms, lips kissing, hands roaming, legs tangling together. She burned and shivered simultaneously at the physical effects of her mind pictures, trembled at the very real way his hands were making her desire him without the stimulus of her erotic imaginings.

"I think you want that too," he was saying.

She did, couldn't he tell that? "I . . ." Brightness burned behind her closed lids, and feeling dazed, she pulled back. The sensual scene that had run riot in her mind faded, and two things registered: She was trembling with need for him, and the lights were coming back on in this section of the park. *Park*. They weren't lying on black velvet making love; they were standing in the park kissing and touching like two teenagers making out on lovers' lane.

Jordan's eyes were glazed with passion as he stared down at her, his expression, like her own, a little dazed. His hair was mussed, as if she'd run her fingers through it, his shirt wrinkled from her being pressed tightly against him. "I can't quite remember how we got here of all places," he told her, smiling slightly and shaking his head as if to clear it. "But I know where I was when I left off. . . ." He trailed off, his pause suggestive. "Any minute there, and I'd have lain you down on the grass and made love to you."

"And I'd have let you," Lori found herself whispering, shocked not just at her words but at having said them aloud.

He reached out a hand to smooth a strand of hair back from her cheek. "That surprises you." It was a statement, not a question.

She realized if she said more, she'd be further exposing her vulnerability, emotional as well as physical. For an excuse she reached for the shawl that had slipped from her shoulders to lie, forgotten, on the grass. Her ears caught the faint splash of water from a nearby pool. "I . . . was going to show you the otters."

"Otters, at a time like this," she heard him mutter behind her, but he followed her to stand and lean on the railing. They watched the animals cavort in the water of their pool, their brown bodies sleek and shining. Occasionally one would chase the other, nipping playfully at a nose or a tail. Then the play was turning to something quite different. Lori's face flamed. First the swans, now the otters. . . .

"It's a night for love." Jordan's voice was soft, seductive against Lori's ear, his words echoing her own thoughts. He cupped her face in his hands and tilted it up to his. His face lowered, and her eyes closed in anticipation of his kiss. Then her eyes were opening, and she was blinking in surprise as his teeth closed ever so gently on the tip of her nose.

Her confusion faded, and she blushed fiery red as a splash in the pool at their side reminded her that the love-nip on the nose was the male otter's preliminary sexual advance.

"Just imitating him," Jordan told her with a laugh, jerking his head in the direction of the otters. He chuckled even more as her blush deepened. The male sat on his haunches, eyes bright with curiosity, whiskers twitching as he sniffed the air trying to identify his visitors by their scent.

"I think we'd better go," she told him, having difficulty now keeping her face straight at his teasing. "Otherwise your friend there won't thank you for interrupting him trying to learn something else from him. Not that . . ." She stopped.

"Not that I need to learn any more?"

On their way out of the park they encountered the guard on duty making rounds with a flashlight. "Hello, folks, just checking to see if the lights came back on in this section. We've had them going on and off all night; must be a short."

The guard peered at her. "Oh, it's you, Lori; didn't recognize you at first. I haven't seen you since I went on night duty."

"I don't usually come here at night," she told him, explaining, "We saw the swans as we drove past and stopped for a moment. Jordan hasn't been here before." She introduced the two men.

"Well, enjoy looking around. I'd better check out the lights in the rest of this section."

The two men nodded, said the usual social pleasantries and Carl left them. Jordan caught up with Lori, who was hurrying to the car.

"I'd forgotten how small towns are. Everybody really does know everybody else here."

She glanced at him, grimaced. "And everybody else's business. Thank goodness he didn't come along sooner."

"We were only kissing, Lori."

"Were we?" She remembered how his hands had roamed all over her body, inflaming her senses.

"Nothing more happened. Yet," he added softly.

Jordan parked the car in the drive and then insisted on walking her to her door, even when she told him he didn't have to do so. She wondered if he hoped he'd be invited inside. I don't know if I can—if I *want* to—say no if he asks to stay the night with me. I've never felt like this, never wanted a man as much as I want him. But it's too soon. "I—I'd invite you in, but it's late," she said as she fitted her key into the lock. She was reminded of the way he felt about people making excuses. "I just . . . I mean, it isn't that I don't want to . . ." She fumbled for words, stared at the key, wondering why it wouldn't work, wishing it would.

Taking the key from her, he turned it right side up, inserted it in the lock and opened the door. Then he placed the key back in her hand and folded her fingers back around it.

"So long as it isn't because you don't want to invite me in for the night," he told her. He plucked the shawl she held in nerveless fingers, held it in his hands behind her head, letting the breeze billow it around her.

"Shall I spin you a veil to protect you tonight?" he asked, a wry smile on his lips. At the question in her eyes, he reminded her of the parrot fish that spins a transparent cocoon in which to sleep each night to keep itself safe from predators. He slid the wrap around her shoulders and tied the ends in a loose knot at her breasts, his fingers lingering for a moment to brush against their softness. His kiss on her lips was swift and sudden and hard. "I can wait for another night with you, until you're ready, Lori. *Somehow*, I can wait. 'Night." He turned and left her.

Lori let herself in and locked the door behind her with hands that shook.

4

thought I'd find you here."

Lori looked up from leaning over Aphrodite's tank to see Jordan striding into the enclosure. "Hi." She watched him a little warily as he sat beside her, his closeness reminding her of his kiss last night and of his enigmatic words about "waiting" for her. Not wanting him to see her reaction to him, Lori turned her attention back to Aphrodite again. She frowned as the dolphin swam listlessly around the tank, paying little attention to her and none to Jordan.

"Lori?"

She sat back on her heels and glanced at him. "What?"

"Something wrong?"

"Of course not. Thank you for dinner and the cruise last night."

"I enjoyed it too." He was silent for a moment. "I have tickets for the band shell concert tonight. Will you go with me?"

"I have to work late. Really," she added, remembering how she'd tried to refuse his date the day before and his request that she be honest and not make excuses why she couldn't go if it was just that she didn't want to do so. The real reason was she had two lessons after work, so she hadn't told the exact truth—but then she couldn't, could she?

"Why do I get the feeling something's wrong?" Jordan mused quietly at her side. "Neither of you is acting your usual self this morning."

Lori poked around in the bucket of fish, searching for just the right one with which to tempt Aphrodite. "Nothing's wrong with me. Andy told me that Aphrodite wouldn't eat for him. I came to see if I could get her to, and I need to be getting to work, Chad's already . . ." She stopped, realizing she'd nearly told him Chad was already upset with her for the quality of a report she'd typed for him, so she didn't want to add to that by coming in late.

"Chad's what?"

"Nothing, he's just used to having his office to himself, and I know I distract him by just being there, let alone coming in after he has." That was true, even if, again, it wasn't the whole truth.

"You're sure that's all?"

Lori nodded, not about to tell him what a silly, adolescent reaction she was having to him the morning after—a mere kiss.

Appearing somewhat reassured, Jordan knelt on

the edge of the tank, unmindful that the knees of his slacks were getting wet. He reached down to put his hand beneath Aphrodite's chin, raising it so that he could look in the dolphin's eyes. "Do you think she might be getting sick?"

"I'm not sure."

"Here, let me try."

"Oh, would you?" She gave him a grateful smile as she handed him the fish. She nearly laughed at the bemused look with which he received it, as if he didn't quite know what reaction he should have about having a dead fish in his hands at this hour of the morning.

"Do you think I should call the vet?"

"I'm probably just worrying for nothing. She's eating for you now." Glancing at her watch, Lori chewed at her bottom lip. "Do you have time to feed her the rest of it? It's past time for me to be at work."

"Relax, even if Chad complains, I'll explain to the boss," he teased.

Edging away from the tank, she said, "I've really got to go." Turning, she slipped out of the enclosure before he could stop her.

She was in the midst of Chad's report, typed at the agonizingly slow rate of four pages an hour, when a voice interrupted her concentration and her fingers slipped, jamming two keys together. "Damn!" she muttered before glancing up.

"You forgot to answer me this morning," said Jordan, perching on a corner of her desk. "About the band shell concert."

"I said I have to work late tonight," she hedged,

reaching to unstick the keys. "I promised Chad I'd finish this report for him before I left. I begin a week's vacation tomorrow, remember?"

"We could skip dinner if you run late and get something after the concert."

She felt his hand beneath her chin, and he was lifting it, staring down intently into her face as he had Aphrodite's. "Lori?"

"Oh, okay."

"Please, try to contain your excitement at going out with me. Such behavior is unseemly in an office."

Lori found herself laughing at the dryness in his voice, and then he was laughing too. "It's just that I have to get this done," she said by way of explaining her lack of enthusiasm and absorption in the task. "Couldn't use the darned word processor."

"You're not working through your lunch hour, are you?"

Moving her chin from his hand, she returned her attention to the keys, finally getting them unstuck. "Uh, no, I'm just waiting for Betsy." *How* was she going to get rid of him before the woman came? Oh, well, Betsy was usually late.

"Maybe I should leave," he said as she began typing.

She looked up and smiled. "It is a little hard to concentrate, and my typing's bad enough as it is."

"Since you said I make it hard for you to concentrate, I'll let you throw me out." He leaned down, and his lips were only a fraction of an inch from her own when they heard a commotion at the door and drew apart.

Betsy bounced into the office, calling, "Hi, ready for

the lesson— Oh!" She stopped in her tracks, gulped as she saw Jordan sitting on Lori's desk. "Uh, hi, Mr. Stark."

"Jordan, please, Betsy," he corrected her with an easy grin.

Once Betsy had confessed to Lori that she thought Jordan "luscious," and now, a little dazzled by his grin and his friendliness, she smiled and said, "Okay. Jordan."

"Are the kids ready, Betsy?" he asked her with a deceptive casualness. Only Lori saw the way his hand clenched at his side.

Betsy didn't take her eyes from his face. If she had, she would have seen Lori's strained features, seen her gesturing to watch what she said. But, trusting soul that she was, Betsy didn't grasp that Jordan's intensity was a danger sign. He waited, still, not betraying himself, reminding Lori again of the way she'd compared him to a shark, waiting, watching, ready to swoop in and gobble you up when you made one unwary move. . . .

"I *told* Lori you wouldn't mind letting us continue in our own time if she just asked!" Convinced she'd been right, Betsy finally turned her attention to her friend and former co-worker and her face went slack. "You . . . didn't ask him." She gulped comically again when Lori shook her head.

"I, uh, I think I hear someone calling me," said Betsy, backing out of the room.

Jordan stood. "I'll see you in my office the minute you're finished with the lesson, Lori," was all he said, and then he was stalking out the door, ignoring her calls to him.

Betsy bombarded her with questions when she arrived at the tank a few minutes later. "Did he hit the roof? Oh, golly, I bet you're mad at me for running out on you like that. I acted like a rat deserting a sinking ship."

"Relax and stop biting your nails. No, Jordan didn't hit the roof, and I can hardly call you a rat when I was the one who talked you into this, now can I? I just hope . . ." She broke off as something occurred to her. She hadn't endangered her friend's job, had she? It was one thing to get yourself fired, quite another to be the cause of a friend's losing her job.

Betsy, ever alert, pounced on her unfinished sentence and worried expression. "You just hope what?"

"I just hope he'll be reasonable and let us go on doing this in our spare time, that's all," she lied smoothly. She didn't want to alarm Betsy when there might not be any reason to do so. So far Jordan had asked only to see her. Maybe it would stop there. . . . She'd take full responsibility, tender her resignation if necessary, but she'd try to make him see Betsy hadn't been guilty of more than good intentions. Damn it, so had *she!* she thought, suddenly getting angry.

Afterward she wondered if she hadn't made things worse for herself by not quite concealing her feelings better. If she had, then maybe she would have been a little more humble, a little more conciliatory. Instead, the minute she'd been shown into Jordan's office by his secretary, she'd been on the defensive, blurting out, "We only did it during our lunch hours and after work. We didn't cost the facility one cent, and—"

"You look exhausted, and you were having to redo a report," he interrupted her. "I checked with Chad while you were giving your lesson, and if I had done the same about Betsy's work, I bet I'd have found her work's been slipping too. I—"

"Please, keep Betsy out of this," Lori begged, the introduction of her friend's name into the conversation serving to remind her that someone else might pay for her actions too. "I talked her into it. Take it out on me, not her."

Her glance shifted from the pencil he held in his hands, which threatened to snap, to the paper she clutched in her own. Smoothing it, she handed it to Jordan. "I typed this out after you left. I figured I'd save you the trouble of firing me."

She watched him as he set down the pencil and unfolded the paper. He scanned its contents. Then he was handing it back to her. "Read it."

Puzzled, she did so, quickly skimming it. She was appalled at the misspellings, the typing, but most of all, the fact that it didn't quite make sense. "I was upset," she muttered. "I don't normally do this quality of work."

"See that you don't in the future."

"You mean—?"

"I'm not firing you. I'm just hoping you won't make it something I ever have to consider."

Lori took a deep breath. "What about the kids?"

"What about them?"

"Well, I can't just forget about them until the grant . . ."

He stood. "I suggest that you do forget the children for the time being, or when the grant comes through, you might not be able to use it. You're burning the candle at both ends, and you're not doing your job well. As director here I can't allow that to go on. Is that clear?"

"Perfectly," she said through clenched teeth. "Thank you," she added as an afterthought.

"You're welcome. Now, I have work to do, and so do you."

As she left she distinctly heard the sound of a pencil snapping in two.

She was pouring herself a glass of iced tea when the door bell rang later that evening. Opening the door, she found Jordan on the doorstep. "What—are you doing here?"

"We have a date."

"Yes, but I thought . . . That is, after today I—"

"Those were work problems," he said, and there was a determined thrust to his chin as he stood there, as if challenging her to say she wouldn't go out with him. "It has nothing to do with us when we're away from the facility. Are you going to ask me in to wait since you're not ready?"

Secretly relieved that he'd found a way to settle things, she found herself nodding and holding the door open so that he could step inside. "I'll be ready in a few minutes," she said before starting down the hall.

After how he'd told her they should neatly compart-mentalize their personal and professional lives, Lori was reluctant to say anything about the facility as they drove past it on the way to the concert. A nagging worry about Aphrodite, though, was important enough to risk his displeasure. She broached the subject and waited for his reaction, crossing the fingers of one hand beside her for luck.

"It's probably nothing," she said when he took his eyes from the road for a moment and glanced at her.

"But your intuition's telling you something's wrong?"

She held her breath. Was he one of those who doubted, even mocked, the accuracy of intuition?

"I know what you're thinking, and I don't feel that way at all," he told her. "The more you rely on intuition, the more you're listening to the subconscious mind telling you what the conscious part hasn't picked up on. We'll stop and have a quick look at her."

Lori smiled, relieved, and when he stretched out a hand across the distance that separated them on the front seat of the car, she took it and held it until he needed it to make the turn into the facility.

"I'm glad you stopped by," said Ben, the night watchman, as he let them into the front gate. "That Aphrodite just isn't acting right. She's usually one of the perkiest ones, always happy to see me when I come on duty. I was thinking about calling you to ask if she was okay."

Aphrodite was even more listless than she had been when Lori had left work. The dolphin's usually bright eyes were dull, and she barely paid attention to Lori and ignored the men. Jordan returned to Ben's station to call the veterinarian while Lori knelt on the concrete edge of the tank and talked softly to Aphrodite.

The veterinarian was grim after he examined the dolphin. "A virus," he said. "Keep her isolated, so the others won't catch it. She needs to be watched carefully for the next day or two. Is there someone who can keep an eye on her?"

"I will," said Lori and Jordan at the same time.

The man looked from one to the other but said nothing as he took medication from his bag. He wrote out a list of instructions and left them, telling Jordan to call him if Aphrodite wasn't better in the morning.

Jordan thanked him and turned to Lori. "Here, take my car keys and—"

"I'm staying," she said firmly.

Shaking their heads, the night watchman and the veterinarian left them.

"And I thought we were going to have an evening free of work problems," said Jordan, sighing.

"This isn't work; I want to stay. Aphrodite's very special to me. She's not just the dolphin I work with; she's become a friend. Please?" Lori's voice was earnest, and she laid her hand on Jordan's arm. "Besides, growing up around all the dolphins at the marine park, I could be of some help."

She wasn't sure if it was the logic of what she said or her touch that persuaded him.

"You can stay," he said. "I'd like you to," he added with a smile. He went to get two chairs from an office so that they'd be more comfortable. Some time later he remembered that they hadn't had dinner and, ignoring her protests that she was fine, went in search of some food. Ben stopped by during his rounds and chatted for a few minutes, revealing without prompting how highly he regarded the younger man. Jordan had, she found out, given the mid-fiftyish man a chance to work when other firms had turned him down because he'd had problems with alcoholism. After a time he left, returning with Jordan, their arms loaded with brown paper sacks.

"I had no idea we were camping out," Lori couldn't resist saying as she watched them set up two chaise lounges.

"Well, I went into the all-night grocery for some sandwiches from the delicatessen section, and you know how it is at those kinds of places, they have everything," he said with a deprecating grin.

"And so you bought everything they had."

"Well, I like that, when I was just thinking of your comfort," he told her haughtily, pretending to be affronted. "As for you"—he turned to Ben, who tried to hide his smile at the exchange—"I guess you won't be wanting the fresh doughnuts I picked up for you in the bakery section?"

"I wouldn't think of being so ungrateful as to refuse them after all the trouble you went to in getting them, sir," the man said respectfully, tipping the brim of his uniform cap.

Catching the surreptitious wink the man shot Lori, Jordan complained good-naturedly, "I don't get any respect around here."

"That was really nice, what you did for him, Jordan." Lori settled herself on the thick plastic cushion of the lounge.

"It wasn't any trouble to bring them when I was getting the sandwiches. Here, I found you one of those salad sandwiches as well as a tuna salad. Oh, and a roast beef, just in case you weaken when you see me eating mine."

"I didn't mean you were being nice for buying Ben doughnuts, and you know it. He told me about your hiring him."

Jordan looked up from the contents of the grocery sack. "He got the job because he was qualified, but more importantly, because he showed a sincere willingness to work. Period. No charity, just good business."

"Why don't you want people to know how nice you are?"

"Ruins my reputation. Coffee or a soft drink? I bought both."

"Coffee, thanks." She fell silent for a moment while she stirred powdered creamer and sugar into the cup. "Have you ever read John D. MacDonald's Travis McGee series?" When he nodded, she said, "You remind me a little of McGee. He says he's in the salvage business—not exactly the same kind you were in—but along the way he does it with people, too, like you do."

He chose to let the personal remark pass apparently. "You've read the books?"

"He was Joe's favorite writer, so his books were always lying around our place. One day I picked one up just to see what they were all about, and I was hooked."

That drew them into a discussion over which was their favorite McGee book, Jordan as much a fan as Joe and Lori since he'd moved to Florida, where the fictional McGee sleuthed while residing on a houseboat. Another similarity, thought Lori. Jordan lived on his cabin cruiser at the local marina.

They ate, then talked, and talked some more as they watched Aphrodite and got her to accept her medication. The moon was bright overhead; the soft splash of Aphrodite in her tank and the waves washing the shore in the distance were the only sounds to be heard. Lori couldn't imagine anyplace she'd rather be, anyone she'd rather be with.

After a time, despite over-stimulation by the caffeine in the countless cups of coffee they drank, the stimulating company of the man in the lounge beside her and the need to stay awake to keep an eye on Aphrodite, Lori found her head nodding.

A splash of water awakened Lori, and she blinked for a moment at the pale light of dawn breaking over the sea, wondering what she was doing lying outdoors on a chaise lounge dressed in the clothes she'd worn last night, a soft blanket tucked up to her chin. Jordan stood in the shallow end of Aphrodite's tank, his arms wrapped around the dolphin in an attempt to keep her blowhole above water. In an instant Lori had thrown off the blanket, kicked off her shoes and joined him, shivering a little in the cool water.

"She's not—worse?"

But it was all too obvious that she was. Aphrodite's usually bright eyes were dull as she stared sadly at Lori, and she was making little effort to keep her head above water. And if she didn't do that, if she couldn't rise to the surface every five or six minutes for air, she'd drown as surely as any human or other mammal who stayed beneath the surface for too long.

"She's going to get better, Lori, I *promise* you."

Lori wanted to cry, You can't promise that! But the more she stared into his eyes, the more she believed it would be so—he'd make it so!

Together supporting the dolphin on each side with

their arms, they "walked" her, keeping her blowhole above water. Again and again they made a circuit of the tank, pausing every now and then to see if Aphrodite could stay afloat herself. If there had been other dolphins with her in the tank, or out in the wild, they'd have performed the same loving task to help one of their kind, but the veterinarian had said not to risk infecting another dolphin, and so Lori kept walking her with Jordan.

"Try, baby, please try," Lori coaxed, and Jordan added his cajolery, too, both of them urging medication on her at the prescribed times.

The sun showed a brighter light over the rim of the sea in the distance. Jordan glanced over at Lori, and she looked away from the sympathy she saw on his face. "Lori, don't cry."

"I'm all right; I'm not crying." But at his gentle concern, the tears began falling faster onto Aphrodite's head, which shone pearly gray in the dawn light. "She's got to get better; she's got to, Jordan! I can't lose her, too. I've lost everyone and everything that ever mattered to me, and now—now—" When his hand touched her shoulder, it was nearly her undoing. "I'm not doing her any good by getting upset." She sniffed, struggling to gain control of herself. "You're not getting tired, are you?"

"No. You?" His expression was kind, concerned.

Lori shook her head.

"I'll walk all next week if it'll help," he told her.

His quiet words were the lifeline she needed. When Andy and Betsy and some of the other staff members stopped by a little later, evidently tipped off by the watchman that one of the dolphins was seriously sick, they offered to spell Jordan and Lori. But Lori refused to leave even for a minute, and Jordan insisted he'd stay until *she* rested. The group walked away, and like the veterinarian and the night watchman, shook their heads at the stubborn twosome.

5

Just when Lori thought she was going to drop from exhaustion, when Jordan looked close to it himself, Aphrodite began swimming on her own.

"Jordan, I can't believe it," she whispered. Brushing back a strand of hair that clung to her cheek, Lori watched Aphrodite dip beneath the water and emerge again a minute later. "You're going to be all right!" she cried, exuberantly throwing her arms around the dolphin, giving her a hug. Releasing her, she turned to Jordan and did the same, quickly, without thought, pressing her cheek against his chest. "Jordan, she's really going to be all right!" Then, realizing what she'd done, she let go of him and stepped back.

He gazed down at her, and she thought she'd never seen a smile as wide and wonderful. "I told you she would be."

"You did. Thank you." She reached up to kiss him.

But what began as a thank you kiss turned into something quite different as their mouths met. His was cool and wet from the water that had splashed on their faces as they'd walked Aphrodite, but in seconds it was warm, warmer, burning, hungry on hers, searching, seeking, drawing all response from her as his arms wrapped around her and they stood in the middle of the tank, all else forgotten.

His hands moved over her breasts, hips, thighs, and heat burned through her wet clothes, which were clinging to her like a second skin. Finding it difficult to slide a hand inside her blouse, he cupped the softness of her breasts in his hands.

Lori touched his damp hair, ran her hands down his neck, his shoulders, over a chest covered with a shirt that defied her seeking fingers. Then he was grasping her hips and pulling her body closer to his, so intimately that it felt as if nothing would prevent their flesh from fusing.

Their kiss raged on, until she told herself if they didn't break their embrace, the water would surely boil. She pulled back from his arms, and his gaze scorched her as it swept over a shirt she saw had turned transparent when wet, over slacks that outlined every curve of her hips and thighs. In the dark of night he'd seen nothing, but today he saw everything. His look was frank and full of desire. He reached for her, and she fairly ran from him, climbing out of the tank. She hurried over to take a towel from a storage cabinet and wrapped it around herself. "Here, you'd better dry off before you catch cold!" she said, handing him a towel when he followed her out of the tank.

He dried his hair with it, his eyes never leaving hers, patting his wet clothes in a vain attempt to dry them. "We should get home and get out of these."

"Yes," she said, blushing at the innuendo. Whose home? she heard an inner voice jeer.

"Here, put this on." He wrapped another towel around her shoulders. "You can't walk through the facility to the parking lot like that or every man in the place will be after you."

Lori's cheeks flamed with color at his words and his husky tone. His eyes were hot and black, still glowing with an inner fire that threatened to blaze out of control again.

They heard footsteps and drew back as Betsy entered. "Hi," she said. Then, as if just realizing what their being out of the water meant, she looked into the tank. "Aphrodite, you're better!" she cried happily, bending down to pat the dolphin's head. She stood, turned to Jordan. "Gee, I almost forgot," she told him. "You have a long distance call from some foundation. I was talking to your secretary when it came in, and I said I'd come get you since I wanted to see how Aphrodite was doing anyway."

Jordan hesitated, as if torn between Lori and the call. Finally he reached into his pocket and handed Betsy his car keys. "Drive Lori home for me, will you?" he asked her. "This call might take awhile, and I don't want her catching cold. I'll see you later, after we've both had a chance to get some rest," he said to Lori. Then he was gone.

Andy came in practically on his heels, saying Jordan had passed him and sent him to keep watch on Aphrodite. Lori knew the dolphin would be all right for a while without her. Besides, she couldn't stay in her soaked clothes, as Jordan had pointed out. And maybe it was better if she left before Jordan returned and took her home himself. After the scene in the tank, she had a feeling he'd want to follow it to its logical conclusion. Yes, it was definitely better to go now.

Grabbing at her purse, Lori turned to Betsy. "Let's go; I'm dying to get home and crawl into bed for some sleep."

"Sure you wouldn't rather wait for Jordan, so he can crawl in with you?" asked Betsy. "Not that you'd get much sleep. But who'd care?"

"You're something else, Betsy Pomeroy. Just what I'm not sure," Lori told her wryly as they headed out to the parking lot.

As it happened, Lori didn't get any sleep even though Jordan wasn't in the bed with her. She tossed and turned, remembering. . . . This man drew her, not just physically, but emotionally, into his thrall, and she didn't know how to deal with what she was feeling. Finally, despairing of sleep, she showered and dressed in jeans and a shirt, plaited her hair in a braid to keep it out of her way in the breeze that was always brisk near Aphrodite's enclosure, and headed back to the facility.

She was sitting there on the chaise where she'd spent so many hours the night before, sipping a cup of coffee bought from a machine in the employees' lounge, when a shadow fell over her.

"Tell me I'm not seeing what I think I'm seeing."

Lori jumped guiltily, spilling a little of the coffee. "Oh, hi, Jordan."

"'Oh, hi, Jordan,'" he mimicked a little sarcastically, standing over her, his hands on his hips. "Are you going to try to tell me you didn't sneak back here after I sent you home for some rest?"

"No."

"You didn't sneak back? You're sitting here; I'd consider that pretty good proof."

"No, I meant, No, I won't try to deny the obvious."

"Andy was supposed to watch her."

"I told him I could manage, so he went back to his work. Aphrodite and I don't need anyone."

Jordan hunched down to sit on his heels beside the chair, and Lori shifted a little uncomfortably on her chair as he brought his face level with hers—and entirely too close. "Now, what's that supposed to mean?"

"Nothing. It's just that no one else needs to watch her; I can do it now that she doesn't need to be supported in the water, that's all." She looked away. "Besides, I just couldn't sleep until I was positive she was absolutely well."

"Fine, Aphrodite doesn't need anyone to help her in the water anymore, and you don't need sleep. Is there anything else you've decided the two of you don't need? Like maybe me?"

Lori glanced sharply at him, then away, feeling a blush creeping into her cheeks.

"Your face is so expressive," said Jordan with a soft chuckle before she could frame a reply. "Especially your eyes. You don't have to answer me; I can see you don't know what to say. I do know one thing, though. I know there's something I need; I knew it from the first time I met you."

"What—what's that?" she asked, unconsciously licking her lips as they went dry while he continued to look at her.

"This."

Before she quite knew what was coming, his mouth was swooping down, capturing hers. She told herself she wouldn't give him any response, that she wouldn't let happen what had happened in that tank only an hour ago. But he was getting that response from her, although gently this time. No, it wasn't something that was his, or hers, to summon up, she realized. This came from someplace that wasn't even a conscious part of them, a place where need dwelled, need so deep that it couldn't even be separated into slots labeled *physical* and *emotional*.

The cup slipped from her senseless fingers, and without breaking the kiss, Jordan was joining her on the lounge, his virile body warm and hard against hers, pressing her deeper into the cushions.

"So sweet, so responsive," he murmured as he pressed a kiss into the corner of her mouth, brushed his mouth across her cheek and then delicately traced the shell-like whorl of her ear with his tongue. "Is this what you were afraid of this morning, Lori? That we'd kiss and this would happen? That then I'd take you home, into your bed and make love to you and never let you out of it?"

Her fingers tightened on his shoulders, and she wasn't sure herself if she meant to push him away or draw him closer. He didn't wait for an answer, but kissed the pulse beating at the base of her throat. His hands roamed over her body. One unbuttoned her shirt and slipped inside to caress her breast, his thumb gently stroking a nipple that hardened to the unexpected, erotic touch. The other hand stroked the soft curves of her hip and thigh. Her conscious resistance vanished; the subconscious need for more of this delicious agony/pleasure was the only thing that registered.

"Tell me you don't enjoy the way I make you feel," he whispered, his voice husky, full of desire.

He was trying to make her admit that she was falling under his potent spell. Were her feelings, was her response, that transparent, that desperate?

Sensing her uncertainty, he said, "Are you still going to say you don't want me after that kiss?"

"One—one kiss doesn't prove anything," she told him breathlessly.

"Then I'd better keep kissing you until I prove my point," he told her, and his mouth came nearer.

There was a splash, and Jordan lifted his head, scowling over his shoulder at Aphrodite. "Thanks a lot, girl! I might need a cold shower, but not out here." He reached down to brush the dampness from his trouser leg, and it was then that Lori realized there was something different about his clothes—he was dressed in the gray suit she'd seen him in the first day he'd come here.

"Do you have a meeting or something?"

"Or something. I'm going out of town." He returned his attention to her, moving back atop her, twining his legs with hers.

"Then . . . shouldn't you be going?" That strange breathlessness was coming over her again.

"Soon."

"What if—what if she splashes more water on you? Hadn't you better get up?"

"Don't you put her up to any more mischief," he warned with a twinkle in his eyes. Then he sobered. "Admit it, Lori. Maybe Aphrodite's kind doesn't need man for his friendship or his love. But you're a woman, darling. Don't turn your back on your need for me, and I don't mean a physical one. None of us is put on this earth to be so independent we don't turn to our own kind for friendship and for love. When you're really lucky, you meet the one who can satisfy that deeper need for love. I can recognize that in you, even if you can't. You have such a capacity for loving; I've seen that with the children in your project and with Aphrodite." He sighed, touched his forehead to hers. "I wish I could understand why love scares you so badly, Lori. Why I do."

"Don't be silly," she told him, moving restlessly beneath him. "You don't scare me. Nothing much does."

"No?" He got up, brushed at his suit. "I'd like nothing better than to debate that with you, but I haven't got the time. I have to catch a plane to Washington."

"Washington? Why?"

"Never mind. Do I get a kiss or not?"

She was feeling the effect of their kisses, and she knew he knew it. His knowing glance as he slid his arms around her waist to steady her as she stumbled a little getting up from the chair forced her to look at him and ask pertly, "Do you need one?"

"You bet I do, and I'm not afraid to admit it," he said, and his kiss was quick and passionate.

"Promise me you'll let Andy or someone else sit with Aphrodite today so you can get some rest."

Lori nodded, crossing her fingers behind her back. He leaned down to give Aphrodite an affectionate pat, and then he was gone.

"I really don't need him," she told the dolphin.

Aphrodite regarded her silently, and Lori stood there, wishing she could better understand what was behind that mysterious Mona Lisa-like smile etched for all who saw to wonder why she looked so. . . .

Jordan found her the next afternoon, sitting in nearly the same place.

"Damn! I'm not believing you! You're just determined to disregard my wishes, aren't you!"

Lori shrank back against the cushions of the lounge. "No, Jordan, I did leave for a rest! Besides, it's not like I've got anything better to do," she pointed out. "I'm on vacation, remember?"

"Some vacation, some rest!" he scoffed, scowling at her. "I can see how long this rest of yours was by the circles under your eyes!"

"Well, you didn't get any rest either, taking off to Washington!"

"That was different."

"Oh? How?"

"Never mind. Come on, there's only one way to get you to take a rest so we'll both get some, and that's to put some distance between you and Aphrodite here! I know you won't mind, will you, girl?" he asked the dolphin, who answered him with a cheerful sound, nodding her head in agreement. Effortlessly lifting Lori into his arms, Jordan strode from the enclosure, calling over his shoulder to a gaping Andy to take care of the dolphin. "Not that she still needs it anymore, but keep an eye on her just to reassure Florence Nightingale here," Jordan added.

"Let me down, you big oaf!" she demanded. "Did you see a Tarzan movie on the plane or something? Where are we going? Answer me, darn you!"

"We're taking a little cruise," he said, answering one of her questions. "I'm going to see to it that you relax and get some rest before you drop." He put her into his car and went around to the driver's side.

"I don't want—"

"I'll carry you aboard bodily if I have to," he warned. A glance at his expression told her he probably would—and enjoy every minute of it! She shut up, glaring at the dashboard, ignoring him as he started the car and drove. He stopped the car at the marina and got out to come around to her side. "Well, which is it?" he asked politely, the twinkle in his eyes confirming her opinion that he was enjoying his little domineering act. "Willing or not?"

Lori looked out the car window, saw people moving around on their boats. She got out, muttering beneath her breath. "I don't see *The Florida Queen.*"

"We're going on my boat," he told her, smiling and waving to his neighbors as they walked down the dock to his boat slip.

"This is called kidnapping, you know!" she said some time later, after hours had passed and still Jordan wouldn't head back to the marina.

"You came willingly," he told her easily, glancing over his shoulder at her as his strong, tanned hands held them steady on their course.

Lori shielded her eyes against the sunlight sparkling off the sea around them, an endless blue stretch in every direction. We must be miles out, she thought, wishing she hadn't been so occupied looking below his boat, a 41-foot Morgan sloop, Freedom, that she hadn't realized they'd left the Intracoastal Waterway and headed out to sea. The sun was warm on her shoulders, the salty tang of the breeze invigorating. In short, everything was perfect. Except for the way Jordan had gotten her here.

"You used false pretenses! You said we were going for a short cruise!"

"We are."

"We've been out for hours! How much longer are we going to stay out?"

"Three days."

"Three days!" she shrieked. "Why don't we just go to Hawaii for the heck of it!?"

"Oh, okay," he said agreeably, reaching for a map. "Would you rather go there than the Keys?"

"Jordan Stark, how could you possibly think I'd want to go off for a whole weekend just like that?" For emphasis, she snapped her fingers. When he didn't answer, she counted to ten and tried again to make him see reason. "Jordan, I don't go off on weekends with men. I haven't even—" She blushed scarlet as she caught his acute interest. "I— Will you take me back?"

"I'll think about it."

" 'I'll think about it,' " she mimicked crossly, stomping away.

"Did you say something, Lori?" he called.

"Not a thing, Jordan! Not a blasted thing!" She

thought she heard his low laugh, and she fumed, thinking that he sounded as if he were enjoying the whole thing. How dared he—well, if not kidnap, then practically force her into coming aboard—and then act as if he'd done nothing wrong? she asked herself indignantly. Why, it was as if the man thought he was a—a pirate!

She sat again in a deck chair and studied him. Yes, she decided, he'd have been one if he'd been born two hundred years earlier. His feet planted apart on the deck, his stance easy and relaxed at the helm, he was a man as thoroughly at home at sea as others were on land. He'd evidently changed from his suit before he'd come to the facility and found her. Although he was dressed all in white—jeans and shirt and deck shoes—the look he sent her over his shoulder was darkly piratical, a look that would have reminded anyone of the brigands who had roamed these very waters plundering ships of their cargoes. And carrying women off, as well.

Lori shivered a little, although she was quite warm. She'd never felt very safe with Jordan when on land. At sea she was even more at his mercy. . . .

The "burning the candle at both ends," as Jordan had put it, was beginning to take its toll on her. Lori felt a sense of lethargy stealing over her as the motion of the boat combined with the warm sun to lull her. That morning the vet had told her that Aphrodite had made a near miraculous recovery. He'd praised the nursing Lori had done. But she knew that Jordan had been the one responsible for the dolphin's recovery. If he hadn't acted as quickly as he had, if he hadn't been awake when Aphrodite floundered, the dolphin might have drowned. And more than knowing what to do, Jordan had known what to say, too, when Lori had thought that she was losing Aphrodite.

She'd had to revise her initial opinion about Jordan, not just because of the way he'd been about Aphrodite, but for so many other reasons. Swimming against a tide of exhaustion, she tried to keep her eyes open. She might have changed her mind about him, but she had to change his about taking her home. Along with the memory of his understanding, sympathy and support in the tank with Aphrodite had come the remembrance of what had happened afterward, of how they had kissed so passionately. . . . She drifted off.

A voice buzzed near her ear saying something about too much sun. Strong arms lifted her, carried her below deck. Too tired to fight, not really wanting to anyway, when it was so nice to snuggle closer to the warmth of another human body that had the most marvelous scent of sea and men's soap and the special male fragrance of Jordan's skin.

He bent over her as he lay her on the bed, and his hands tugged at her clothes. "You'll be more comfortable without these."

Drowsily she tried to form a protest, tried to stop his undressing her, but before she could, the clothes were gone and a light blanket was being pulled up over her. She subsided, realizing he wasn't making amorous advances, but she couldn't help muttering, "too darned high-handed. . . . Think you always . . . know what's best." Subsiding into the delicious comfort of the bed, she returned to the dream state between consciousness and sleep. Her last conscious thought up on deck returned, and she must have said something aloud, for Jordan was chuckling. "So I'm a pirate, eh? Well, sometimes I admire the way they went after what they wanted, regardless of risk!"

She drowsed, thinking he'd left the room. Hearing his voice again, she blinked disbelievingly at the sight before her. Was she dreaming?

"Aye, a pirate, and bewitched by a mermaid, I am!" Jordan was saying, and his rich laughter filled the cabin. He stood at the end of the rough wooden bed upon which she lay, his legs braced against the rolling of their vessel. Dimly she heard the creaking of timbers, saw the changing light from an oil lamp that swung on a chain over his head cast patterns of light and shadow over his features. He was dressed as she'd never seen him before—or rather, undressed, as he divested himself of the sword and scabbard at his broad belt. The wide-sleeved white broadcloth shirt, long leather boots and breeches of soft brown fabric that hugged his muscular thighs followed.

Then he was lowering himself to the bed beside her, his lips plundering the sweetness of hers, his hands moving on her body, searching, stroking, ravishing. His lovemaking was bold, demanding a response as ardent and unrestrained as his, and what he awoke in her was like nothing she'd ever experienced with the one man for whom she'd ever cared enough to even think about sharing such intimacies of body and soul. She touched him, tentatively at first, soon finding that no matter how untutored in the lessons of love she thought she might be, she instinctively pleasured him with her loving eagerness. Unafraid of the sensations their lovemaking sent surging through her, eager for more no matter how she'd once feared showing him how much she needed him in an emotional as well as physical way, Lori eagerly joined with Jordan, and they ventured forth on their quest for fulfillment.

Hovering on the brink, his body about to plunge them toward ecstasy, Lori woke, trembling. She stared wild-eyed around the empty cabin of Jordan's modern boat, not the oak-beamed vessel of her dream.

A dream! Everything had been a dream.

6

A rush of cool air hit Lori's skin as the light blanket that had covered her fell to her waist. Startled, she found she was dressed only in her bikini panties. What had happened to her clothes? She couldn't remember taking them off—Jordan, he'd done it, she recalled with an all-over blush.

Swinging her legs over the side of the bed, Lori pulled the blanket around her, sarong fashion, while she searched for her clothes. They weren't on the bed, or on top of the dresser or in the bathroom. She looked all around the cabin, but they were gone. Where could they be? she asked herself, puzzled.

The boat's engine was silent, and waves gently slapped the hull. Were they finally home? Opening the cabin door, Lori began climbing the steps, hastily drawing back when she glanced up and saw Jordan descending them.

"So you're finally awake," he said, smiling. He handed her a plastic bucket filled with raw shrimp in the shell that glistened in the fading light. "Stow these below for me, will you? They're dinner."

Lori wrestled with the blanket with one hand, trying to stay covered, trying to cope with the bucket with the other hand. "Wait. Where are my clothes?"

"Up on deck. Why, did you want them?" Mischief danced in the depths of his black eyes.

"Of course I want them!"

"Then you'll have to wait; I have other things to get." He took the stairs in two effortless strides.

Setting the bucket in the galley sink, Lori stomped up the steps. "Really, Jordan, to take my clothes up. . . ." She stopped, aghast. A man stood on the dock where Jordan's boat was moored, a man who was clearly enjoying her dishabille.

"Nice to see you again, Jordan! You, too, miss!" the man called, tossing Jordan the mooring ropes.

Cheeks flaming, Lori beat a cringing retreat. "How could you do that to me? How could you?" she demanded when Jordan entered the cabin a little later.

"Here, this is for you."

Instinctively she caught the bag he tossed and promptly lost the blanket covering her.

"What would you have done if you'd woke up and found I'd docked?" he parried, folding his arms across his chest and leaning in the doorway to watch her drop the bag as if it were hot coals and frantically reach for the blanket.

Lori hitched the blanket up around her. "I'd have gotten off this blankety boat!"

He laughed. "That's why I took your clothes up on

100

deck after you fell asleep, before I went into the restaurant for our dinner. Open the bag and see if you like what I bought you."

Reaching into the bag printed with "Cap'n Jack's Restaurant—Gift Shop—Bait and Tackle Place," Lori pulled out a long aquamarine caftan of the thinnest gauzy material, a sunny yellow knee-length smock dress, sunglasses and a wide-brimmed straw hat. "Why did you buy these?" she asked, puzzled.

"We didn't get to bring along any of your things, and I didn't think my clothes would fit you. Not that I care if you wear anything," he added hopefully.

She ignored his wistful leer. "Jordan, when are we going home?"

"Not for a while."

"When?"

"As soon as I decide you've had enough rest."

"I've had enough rest."

He merely continued to watch her, infuriating her, and she stomped her foot, stepping on the hem of the blanket and dragging it down so that it hung on the tips of her breasts. Catching his interested look, she yanked it up and tucked it beneath her arms. She opened her mouth, but he was interrupting her, asking, "Do you know how to boil shrimp?"

His question off the subject threw her for a moment. "Of course."

"Good. If you do that, I can take us out to sea." He turned to leave, glanced over his shoulder as an afterthought, and said, "Oh, and wear that caftan thing. Please," he added when she looked as if she might object. Then he left her, closing the door behind him.

Deciding that with the evening air growing cooler, the long-sleeved caftan might be more appropriate than the sleeveless smock dress, Lori pulled it on. Deceptive, that's what the thing was, she thought, catching a glimpse of herself in the mirror above the dresser as she brushed out the tangles in her long hair. Although the garment appeared full and flowing when on, it was quite the opposite, clinging sensuously to every curve. And while she might be covered from her neck to her toes—and wrists—the material was dismayingly diaphanous, and she had no bra to wear beneath, not having had one on beneath the shirt she'd worn aboard. I can't wear this! she thought, and reached for the other dress.

There was a rap on the door. "Lori? Can I come in? I want to show you where things are in the galley." Then he was opening the door and already inside before she could refuse him.

In this thing I'm showing *you* where everything is on me, not that you don't already know by undressing me! she thought, waiting nervously for his reaction. Would he react like the pirate in her dreams?

"I like it," he told her, smiling approvingly, evidently well pleased with his taste. "Although it's a little hard to see in here."

"Never mind the light," she said quickly, brushing past him, grateful he apparently couldn't see through the dress as much as she'd feared. "I think I can find everything." She turned and found that Jordan had followed her. "Besides, it's too cramped in here for both of us."

"Oh, I don't know," he disagreed, his grin wicked as he stared down at her. "I like it."

Lori flattened herself against the counter as he maneuvered past her in the narrow space, filled a large pot with water and set it on the stove for her. He showed her how to start the flame beneath it.

"There's a salad and a bottle of wine in the cooler, a loaf of fresh Greek bread and a Key lime pie in the box on the counter. Will that be enough?"

"It sounds like a feast."

"Good. We'll eat up on deck. If you don't need anything else, I'll go up." But he lingered, watching her.

Feeling a little self-conscious, Lori turned her attention to the pot on the stove. The water had to be boiling by now—it was the stove that was making the kitchen so hot, wasn't it? she asked herself. Her attention on the man so near, she was startled when steam rose as she lifted the lid. She slammed the lid back on, but the pot holder she'd been using slipped, and her finger made painful contact with the metal handle. "Ouch!" she cried, and Jordan was at her side—not that he'd ever been far from it in the galley. He pulled her over to the ice cooler, scooped up a handful of ice and packed it around the burn as he held her hand.

"Better now?" he asked as the ice melted and the water dripped into the cooler.

"Yes, thanks. I'm not usually such a klutz in the kitchen. It'll be fine," she assured him when he continued to hold her hand. "It's only a little burn." She tried to sound light, but her words seemed to vibrate a little. The contact with his fingers, his nearness, disturbed her far more than the minor burn. Unbidden, the memory of their lovemaking in the dream flashed into her awareness. Heat poured over her, and afraid he might somehow feel the blush that covered her from head to toe, she pulled away to pour the shrimp into the boiling water, her back to him.

"Be careful; young tender things burn easily," he cautioned.

She wondered if there was a double meaning to his words, but when she looked up, he'd gone. She heard the throb of the engine a few minutes later, and they were underway again.

Boiling the shrimp was easy. Lori watched their color change from grayish-green to pink, and as they floated to the surface of the water, cooked, she lifted them with a slotted spoon to a waiting bowl. She turned off the burner when the last of them was done and assembled the rest of the meal on a tray. At last everything was ready.

The engine was shut off, and then Jordan joined her in the kitchen. "There you are. I was beginning to wonder what was taking so long. Did it take that long to boil the shrimp?" He took the tray from her, so she followed him, carrying the wine.

"I didn't over-cook them; they'll be quite tender, I assure you." His words about young tender things came back to her. Searching about for something to do as he lifted the food from the tray, transferring dishes to a small table he'd set up, Lori suddenly became aware of the beauty of her surroundings. Bright pink clouds hung in a darkening sky, and the sea all around the boat was a blaze of orange and scarlet, the sun a golden ball sinking into the flame-colored water on the horizon.

"It looks like the water's on fire!" she exclaimed.

"That's not the only thing that is," Jordan muttered.

Following the direction of his stare, Lori glanced down at the caftan, and her eyes widened. The glow from the setting sun was enough to reveal the shadowed outline of her body.

"Hey, where are you going?"

"To change into the other dress."

Jordan's hand shot out to stop her. "Don't, Lori. No, that's not why I bought it," he said, clearly reading her mind. "I bought it because I knew it was your favorite color, and I thought it would look good on you. I never considered its thinness might make it easier to see through."

He even knew what her favorite color was. What doesn't he know about me? she wondered. Does he know how nervous I am about being all alone with him way out here?

"Come on, sit down and eat. It'll be dark soon."

She took a seat at the table, thinking, You're looking at me as if you can't decide on those shrimp—or me! His attention was unnerving and pleasurable all at the same time, a case of wanting to be desired—yet afraid of the price she might pay for it. The feeling wasn't a new one; she'd felt it so often around him.

Too aware of him, knowing she couldn't keep her arms crossed in front of her forever, or even until dark, Lori plucked a shrimp from the bowl and began peeling it inexpertly. He did see you half naked when he took your clothes off and nothing happened, she reassured herself.

"Here, do it like this." Jordan showed her, deftly stripping the shrimp of its transparent shell in one quick motion with a technique she'd never tried. His eyes were steady on her lips instead of her front as he offered her the succulent morsel. But the brush of his fingers on her lips was a sensuous reminder of his kisses, the sight of the empty shrimp shell in his other hand a reminder of the transparency of what she wore—although armor would have been no protection against the sexual attraction that had flared up between them right from the start. Swallowing the shrimp before she'd fully chewed it, Lori choked as a piece lodged in her throat.

Jordan gave her a healthy thump on her back. "Better? Here, have a drink of this to wash it down."

The wine he handed her was cool and dry and pleasing to the palate. "Mmm," she murmured when he asked how she liked it. "It's wonderful." Everything is, she found herself thinking: the sunset, the food, having him all to myself even if I don't quite know yet what will happen. . . . She picked up another shrimp, not really hungry, but it helped to have something to concentrate on besides her thoughts.

"Take it slower; there's no need to rush," he was saying, meeting her eyes levelly. "Not at anything, Lori."

Taking a deep breath, she asked the question that had been bothering her while she prepared dinner. "Where are we, Jordan?" Don't tease, don't say, "On the ocean" or something like that, she prayed silently. Don't take this lightly, please.

"Too far to swim back, but if you want to go back, I'll take you." He paused for a moment, then went on, "I thought we might cruise around the Keys this weekend."

Unable to meet the question in his eyes, her glance dropped to the shrimp she'd picked up. She found herself picking at the shell, toying with the crustacean with no real intention of eating it. "I told you I don't go off on weekends with men," she finally said in a quiet voice.

"Nothing has to happen if you don't want it to, and I mean that, Lori. I want us to have a chance to get to know each other, really know each other."

Still she hesitated. It was no line; he was sincere. But . . .

"You don't have to decide now. I'm hungry; how about you?"

She opened her mouth to answer him, and he popped a shrimp inside before she could. He peeled one for himself, then another for each of them, and she was eating. Enjoying the meal with him became more important than her fears now that he had reassured her he'd take her home if she wanted him to do so. Only she took over feeding herself; the way he was doing it was just a little too . . . intimate for her.

Lori ate, a shrimp, a bite of salad glistening with oil and vinegar dressing, the crusty bread, a sip of wine; a bite of shrimp and salad and bread and another sip of wine; shrimp, bread, wine; shrimp, wine; then, nothing but the lovely sensual slide of the wine down her throat. She felt light and warm and wonderful, the effects of the wine washing over her like the caress of warm water against her skin when she swam, glowing with its effects inside as she felt her skin did when the dawn touched it on those early morning swims she loved.

Sated, they moved from the table. "Oooh, the floor's moving," Lori told Jordan, giggling as she bumped against him.

"It's supposed to; we're on a boat, remember?" he told her with an indulgent smile. He put his arm around her, and they walked to the bow. There he pulled the cushion that was as big as a mattress from the double chaise lounge and threw it down on the deck. "Here, let's sit."

Lori shook her head, going to stand at the railing. The sea breeze moved softly in her hair and the filmy folds of the caftan. She crossed her arms, resting them atop her head, and gazed up at the stars, then out to where their brightness was reflected in the diamantine surface of a gentle night sea. Why, she wondered dreamily, was everything just a little out of focus? Had she really had too much to drink? Did she even care?

Sighing, she said, "This is wonderful. Thank you for all of it, Jordan."

"I can't take credit for the night. I only provided the boat and the food."

And wonderful company, she wanted to add, but hearing the smile in his voice, she turned to face him in the moonlight. She must have had more to drink than she'd thought because he was wearing the smile she'd heard in his voice and she couldn't even remember what her last word had been. "Did I say something funny?"

He shook his head.

"Then what are you smiling at?"

"You." He held out his hand. "Come here, and I'll tell you why."

Lori had only gotten this tipsy once before in her

life. Then she'd been out at a party with Betsy, and her friend had teased her the next morning about how she'd gotten "loosened up" and silly. She was afraid she'd made a fool of herself, but with the kind of regal nonchalance only the truly pickled can affect, she crossed the space between them with a great casualness. "Well?" she asked a little haughtily as he pulled her down beside him on the cushion.

Jordan was really chuckling now. "You were so worried about my seeing through this dress before," he explained, lifting her arm, showing her how the moonlight streamed through the material as clearly as through air, and she didn't have to imagine what he had been seeing when she stood at the railing and at dinner.

"I could promise not to look or touch," he told her quietly. "But I think you know we can't stop what's happening between us that way." He framed her face in his hands, holding it gently, as one might a rare and beautiful shell, as he gazed at her. "You're working a sea spell on me, you know that?" He kissed her, working a magic of his own, one that had Lori under his spell as his hands stroked her hair all the way down her back to where it stopped at the softness of her rounded hips. Both of them were breathless when they drew apart.

"I . . ." Lori began. She shook her head slowly, wonderingly, no longer sure what she'd wanted to say. She felt out of her depth, drifting in dangerous and uncharted currents. Jordan had brought her on a journey, one she sensed she would return from changed, somehow, no matter what course they took next.

He kissed the hollow of her throat, and then his mouth was on hers again, his tongue gently exploring the moistness within, and she was lost to everything, yet found everything in Jordan's arms. In Jordan. Oh, this was what she wanted; she didn't want it to stop; she didn't want to run away anymore.

Her hands went to the neckline of her caftan. A tug of the ribbon released its bow, and the garment slid from her shoulders, baring her breasts. She heard him utter a funny sound she couldn't decide was a moan or a laugh but very probably was both by the expression of delighted disbelief on his face at her action. He caressed her breasts and then his mouth took over the tantalizing, tormenting motions of his hands on one breast, then another, and a stab of longing shot through her, shook her. She wanted more of his touch, wanted to touch more of him. Raising herself up on her knees, she reached for the buttons on his shirt, and as she did, forgot the motion of the boat. She was caught unawares and half fell against his chest.

Jordan's hands shot out to catch her, and as he held her, his eyes searched her face. "You okay?"

"I'm fine. I think," she said, after she had a moment to think his question over. "The boat's making me a little dizzy all of a sudden though," she had to admit.

He shook his head. "That's not it at all. You had too much to drink. I think we'd better forget this tonight."

"Even if I did have a little more wine than usual, I can handle it," she said with some tartness.

His smile was sad. "I told you nothing would happen unless you wanted it, and—"

"I do!" she protested.

"I shouldn't have touched you after what I said, much less let things get to the point they did. I had the feeling you were drinking more than you could hold at dinner. You did it so that it would be easier to let down your inhibitions, to let me close." He sighed. "But what about tomorrow? We'd just go back to what we've had before, two steps forward, one step backward. When you decide that you want a relationship with me, let me know."

He reached out to help her draw the caftan up over her shoulders again, but pride made her back away from him to do the job herself. She got to her feet carefully and he stood, too. The warmth of passion had seeped from her. She felt cold and tired. Disillusioned. Rejected.

"Now what do we do?"

Jordan smoothed a strand of her hair behind one ear. "You're tired and I'm tired. Let's get some sleep, and then you can decide if you want me to take you back in the morning or . . ." He trailed off, and she heard real regret in his voice. Then he was telling her to go below and that he'd sleep on the cushion up on deck. "Go on, it's warm enough tonight and the cushion's soft. I'll be fine up here."

Lori remembered how soft the cushions had been, remembered that and how close they'd come. "I—I'll get you a pillow," she stammered, turning away.

"I'll come with you."

"I'm not falling down drunk, Jordan! I can manage the stairs!" The minute the words were out, she was wishing she could recall them. "I'm sorry."

"So am I, for making you think I don't want you," he said quietly behind her. "I do, Lori. But one night

111

wouldn't be enough. I'd only want more, many more, and at this stage I'm not sure I'd have that if I took what you were offering tonight. Do you understand what I'm saying?"

Lori nodded, then shook her head, nothing very clear in her head right now, and not just because of the alcohol.

"Damn," he said, turning her and gathering her into his arms. "I'm trying so hard not to do anything to hurt you or what we could have together, and somehow I'm doing it in spite of my best intentions." His hands smoothed over her back, soothing her, and after a moment he was setting her from him. "But I've found the right things aren't usually the easy ones to do. If I don't take myself far away from you right now, I'm not going to be able to." He kissed her forehead, grabbed his pillow and blanket and left her to stare after him.

An hour later she was still staring at the empty doorway as she lay huddled in the bed, awake, miserable and stone-cold sober. Deciding there was no point in trying to sleep any longer, she got up and with bare feet tiptoed into the galley. Coffee often kept her awake, but she felt as far from sleep as she could ever remember being, so she fixed herself a mug of instant and sipped it in the galley. The coffee didn't warm her inside, where she was cold, but it cleared her head, dispelling the last of the alcoholic haze and helping her to think.

What she had begun to experience earlier and only now was beginning to understand was what Jordan had been talking about beside Aphrodite's tank that day before he'd left on his trip, she realized. He'd talked about wanting and needing and loving, not just physically but emotionally, too.

Almost without conscious volition, she set down the empty mug and climbed the stairs, her movements like those of a sleepwalker. The caftan she'd worn to bed billowed around her in the breeze as she walked over to the cushion upon which Jordan was sleeping to stand there and stare down at him. He lay on his back, his face relaxed in sleep, his expression more vulnerable than it was when he was awake. She felt something stir deep within her, crying out soundlessly for him, and as if he heard her in his sleep, he opened his eyes. "Lori?"

7

"Can't you sleep?"

Lori shook her head.

"Want to talk?"

Again she shook her head.

He sighed heavily and sat up. "You want me to take you back. Tonight."

"No." Sinking down onto her knees, she rested her hands on his shoulders and kissed him, gently at first, then, taking advantage of his initial surprise to her kiss, she slid her tongue between his parted lips and explored within. Her hands left his shoulders to wrap around his neck, drawing them closer, and they kissed long and deep until she lifted her head to look down at him.

"What I want is to make love with you." She lifted her hands from the back of his neck to run them through his thick midnight-black hair, loving the feel of its silkiness between her fingers. She stared into his eyes, eyes that had the same black sheen, and were gazing intently upon her face.

"Make love with me, Jordan. I'm sober now, and I'm glad you waited, because I do know now what I really want, and that's to make love with you."

Her hands left his hair to trail down his face. Without taking his eyes from hers, he caught one of her hands and pressed a kiss into her palm. Then he was drawing her down to lie with him on the cushion, kissing her again and again and again.

When at last he lifted his head, he smiled down at her, saying, "That was the hardest thing I've ever done in my life, stopping us before. But I'm glad I did. I was hoping for this." And then his mouth was on hers again.

They kissed slowly, lingeringly, desire rising up just as quickly and breathtakingly as before, but deliberately they prolonged their lovemaking so that the final pleasure would be greater than a quick, if passionate, coupling. Just as in her dream, Lori's fears of her ability to arouse him vanished when every touch of her hands on his body had him wanting more, moaning and writhing against her and touching her in even more thrilling ways.

Rising up on her knees, Lori cast off the caftan, and Jordan helped her remove the lacy bikini pants beneath. He ran his hands down her naked body, which gleamed like a soft pearl in the moonlight. He stood, and his silhouette blocked out the stars as he bared his beautiful male body to her blushing gaze, and his readiness for her was revealed.

"No, look at me, know what you're doing to me, Lori," he asked when she looked away, suddenly shy.

She did. "And you to me," she found herself saying, marveling at hearing herself utter such intimate words. She held out her arms, and he joined her again on the cushion.

He lay on his side, his eyes serious as he linked the fingers of one hand with hers. "You're sure this is what you want? It's not too late to turn back if—"

"I don't want to turn back!" She pulled her hand from his, grasped his face and kissed him, moaning against his lips as his hands again explored the softness of her breasts, the firm curve of her hips and thighs, and found how ready she was for him.

"Oh Lori, Lori, what a wonder you are!" His laugh was low, exultant against her neck as he submerged his body in hers and they moved forward on their sensuous journey toward ecstasy.

A rhythm as old as the sea—and as new as this moment—took over, the surging, powerful force that was Jordan leading her into previously uncharted depths of passion. Rapture was building from deep within her body. She was overcome with its sensations, wanted to stay forever in this world of pleasure, but soon found she wanted something more.

They rode a rising wave, cresting in a wild burst of joy that seemed to go on forever, buffeted by waves of ecstasy crashing over them again and again. Lori clung to Jordan to keep from drowning, uncaring if she did, as long as it was with him, until at last they lay quietly together, savoring the last fleeting ebb tides of pleasure.

"No mortal woman makes love like that," he told

her, stroking her body with his hand, and her sensitized skin tingled. "Has Aphrodite been telling you secrets?"

Lori smiled against his chest. Dolphins were not just loving creatures; they were sensuous, freely loving, frequently coupling with their own kind. Aphrodite was so loving, she'd even been named for the goddess of love.

Lying there in Jordan's arms, Lori knew a fulfillment that went deeper than the physical, a communication without words, a bond with this man that was more than she'd ever experienced with any other. She felt a kind of expectant fullness for Jordan that she'd had on a different level, in another kind of love—parent love—for Joe. Am I falling in love with him? she asked herself. She forced the thought away, afraid to examine it.

Much later, when Jordan felt her drowsing against him, he swept her up in his arms, saying, "No falling asleep. I have plans for you, my treasure," as he carried her below to his bed.

A kiss on her closed eyelids woke Lori. That, and the hand that stroked her bare shoulder. "Wake up, sleepyhead," Jordan murmured close to her ear.

"Jordan, not again!" she pretended to complain, trying to pull the sheet up over her head. "I thought you wanted me to get some rest this weekend."

"Didn't you get enough sleep?" He laughed when she pulled the sheet from her face to stare disbelievingly at him.

To Lori it seemed as if she'd just fallen asleep. After he'd carried her below last night, they'd made love again; there in the bed in which she'd earlier tried to sleep alone, she found herself responding as she'd never dreamed she could. Jordan set free all the loving locked inside her with a power that went beyond skilled lovemaking. She was awed and overwhelmed, too lost in the splendor of it to want to analyze her emotions.

And he wasn't giving her time to think this morning.

"*Where* do you get all your energy?" she asked, laughing as he advanced on her to playfully nip at her shoulder with his teeth. He was already dressed in a short-sleeved navy shirt and white shorts, both of which displayed his muscular arms and naked legs to advantage. She was reminded of how he'd looked this morning when they'd fallen asleep just as dawn's light had entered the cabin through the portholes. His arms curved around her, he'd been the first to fall asleep, and with a sense of wonder she'd lain awake on her side facing him, thinking how beautiful he was. There was strength in his well-muscled body, strong passion as they fulfilled their desire, and yet tenderness tempered this strength.

"You're not answering me."

"Mmm, you taste good," he told her, finding more tender places to nip at with his strong white teeth. Lori found herself pressed up against the wooden headboard, coming fully awake as her body began responding to the playful feel of his mouth and teeth on her neck, her breasts, her stomach.

"I . . . Jordan, you said you wanted to get started," she reminded him, gasping as his mouth closed around one nipple, and instead of taking little pleasure nips his tongue shot out and licked it instead.

Groaning, he pushed himself away. "I already *had.* And as much as I'd like staying here with you doing this, I want to do a lot more this morning, lady."

"Like what?"

"You'll see. There's scrambled eggs and toast and coffee in the galley. Get dressed and come on up when you're ready." Leaning over for a last kiss, he whispered, "Last night was wonderful, Lori."

"For—for me too." She thought she'd lost her shyness after revealing herself so intimately to him last night, not just physically but emotionally, but still she blushed. He brushed her cheek with his fingers, sensing her mood and not teasing her.

"There're some swimsuits in the drawer; you should be able to find something to fit, okay?"

He kissed her, and then he got up to leave her. Naked, Lori went to look in the drawer he'd indicated. She felt a faint niggle of something that wasn't strong enough to be suspicion, more a frowning question at why he should have a woman's swimsuit —or more than one, from the way he'd sounded— on his boat. She hesitated, her hand on the drawer knob.

But like Pandora, she had to see what was within. She yanked it open and found it filled with swimsuits of several colors and styles and sizes from a modest white one piece to a bright orange string bikini. How many women have you had on board with you, Jordan? she wanted to fling at him.

"It occurred to me that you might not understand," Jordan said behind her.

"What's to understand?" she asked, striving for a lightness she didn't feel. "I'm old enough to know there were other women before me, and there'll be others after—"

"Stop it!" He grasped her by the upper arms, pulling her to her feet to face him. "I'm not going to let you spoil what's happening between us with your suspicions, do you hear me? I've had guests on the boat occasionally, and sometimes they didn't have a suit either, so now I keep some available. Just as people who own a pool often do. For *both* sexes, Lori. If you'd opened the drawer next to that one, you'd have seen there were suits for men as well." He released her arms and bent to rummage in the rainbow of swimwear. "Here, you can use your imagination to wonder what female wore this!" He tossed a black swimsuit to her, a one piece made of black nylon.

Lori held the suit up to herself and saw that at least two of herself might fit inside it. She glanced up at Jordan, and laughter welled up inside her. "I'm . . . sorry, Jordan. I don't know why it should have bothered me; I mean, I know you've had other women, but . . ." She stopped as Jordan frowned. "I'm getting in deeper, aren't I? But I'm just trying to say that I know you have needs—"

"You," he said as he advanced toward her, plucking up an aqua bikini and exchanging it for the black suit in her hands, "don't know anything about needs. If you did, you'd know what I really need is for you to get some clothes on so we can get underway!"

Eyeing the desire in his eyes, Lori stammered, "Aye, aye, sir!" and beat a hasty retreat to shower and dress.

Later, sipping coffee and nibbling at a piece of toast

(who, Lori wanted to know, could possibly be expected to eat eggs first thing in the morning?), she watched Jordan weigh anchor and start the engine. Nothing more was said about the suits, although she'd noticed his approving look when she came up wearing the bikini.

"Lori, look!" Jordan gestured at the bow, cutting through the waves.

A school of dolphins had joined them. Leaping and diving in the sparkling water, they moved with a graceful power and speed that enthralled both of them. Lori stood with Jordan, who had one arm around her and one hand guiding the helm. Sunlight glinted off the silver bodies as the dolphins played their game of welcome—and challenge—at the bow, for they showed clearly that they matched, were even exceeding, the speed of Jordan's sleek, fast craft.

Lori glanced up at Jordan and found him smiling down at her. Wordlessly they exchanged a look that told Lori he was as glad to be there sharing the special sight with her as she was with him.

"Why do you think they were swimming before us like that?" she asked him when at last they lost their playful entourage.

"Some say it's because the rush of water feels good," he said, "a caress that's almost sensual over their skin. Others think that it's for cleaning purposes. But then still others say that the dolphins could be cleaned or find pleasure as easily by swimming in the wake of a ship."

"But they never swim there," Lori finished for him, and they were silent for a while. Lori found her thoughts drifting. She wondered how long it would be before man learned why these mammals, which had no need for anything from him, which often met peril at man's hand, still let man not only approach—but invited contact!

"Remember how I called you a pirate?" When he nodded, she asked, "Did you ever hear the old legend that dolphins are really pirates? Joe told it to me once."

He hadn't heard it, so she told it to him. "Pirates kidnapped a Greek god, supposedly with the intention of selling him into slavery. He turned their oars into serpents, filled the ship with ivy and commanded invisible flutes to play. The ship couldn't move, held by the vines of ivy, and the sailors were driven mad by what they'd seen him do, by the music he made. They threw themselves into the sea and were transformed into dolphins, and that's why dolphins are friendly to man today."

"Because they're repentant pirates, eh?"

"Right."

"Think I'd become a dolphin if I jumped overboard?"

"You haven't heard any flutes . . ."

"But you were singing in the shower and it was as bad to hear as you said once," he teased, then cried "Ouch!" as she pummeled his arm with her fist. "Besides, you might have called me a pirate, but I'm not repentant. I'm glad I kidnapped you."

"So am I," she said softly, and her grin matched his.

"I miss Aphrodite," she said after a moment, and he nodded.

His black eyes studied her as he stood guiding the

wheel, the wind rippling through hair that glinted blue-black beneath the bright sun. "Lori," he began, then he fell silent.

"What?"

"Nothing. I forgot what I was going to say." He reached to fiddle with a dial beside the wheel, and she shrugged, figuring whatever it was hadn't been important.

Time was a pleasant wash of sunlight and sea.

In the distance they could occasionally catch a glimpse of a Key—island—ringed by coral reefs as they traveled through incredibly blue water. Here and there houses and other signs of human occupation dotted a Key. On some the only inhabitants were the man-o'war birds and other fowl that soared high above palm trees rustling in the trade winds. Lori thought she saw several brown dogs romping along the edge of the wood on one island, and when Jordan handed her a pair of binoculars, she found they were the tiny, fragile-looking Key deer. He told her they'd almost been extinct some time back but now were protected by law so their numbers had grown.

Although Lori had grown up in Florida, she'd never visited the hundreds upon hundreds of islands and reefs that stretched in an arc for some two hundred miles from the tip of the state.

They ate sandwiches made by Lori with last night's shrimp tossed into a salad between slices of crusty bread. Cold bottles of beer she found in the galley's small refrigerator completed the simple but perfect repast.

Some time later that afternoon Jordan guided their passage into the shallow bay of an island and docked.

A familiar call came from the side of the boat, and Lori went to look in the water. A dolphin greeted her.

"Hello," she called down, smiling. Behind her she heard Jordan's footsteps, and then he was sliding his arm around her waist, saying, "I see you've met Misty. Hi, girl, tell Peter we're here, will you?"

"Misty? 'Tell Peter we're here'? Jordan, what's going on?"

"You'll see," was all he'd say. "Come on!" He swung her over the side in his arms, and she was once again reminded of the way he resembled a pirate, taking her with him to—this hideaway island?

All she could see was a stretch of pale-sanded beach on one side and a stand of twisted mangrove trees on the other. When Jordan took her hand, pulling her along, she followed, mystified. Then she saw what the trees concealed, a small, stucco building with a tiled roof. A weathered sign was painted DELPHIS COMMUNI-CATION.

Delphis? Delphinus delphis was the species name for common dolphin, Lori knew.

"Jordan! I didn't expect you for another hour!" a somewhat shy-looking man with sandy hair exclaimed as he opened the door before they could knock.

"We made good time."

"This must be Ms.—"

"Lori," she said firmly, shaking his outstretched hand.

"You've been awarded a rather special privilege, one Peter extends to few people," Jordan told her as they were ushered inside.

Peter's face turned pink, but his light blue eyes shone behind wire-rimmed glasses. "Jordan's told me about what you've been doing with the kids, and I'm impressed, Lori. I told him if you were ever in the neighborhood he should bring you by."

"I called him from the restaurant last night," Jordan explained to her.

What followed was an extraordinary two hours. In the space of that short time, Peter showed her his sole project, an extension of an experiment done years before in which a human and a dolphin lived together in order to develop some form of communication between them. Here Misty, the dolphin that had greeted them as they docked, swam in and out of Peter's facility at will through a special opening directly from the ocean into a pool Peter had built next to his living quarters.

Jordan told Lori he hoped they'd be able to do something similar one day at the facility where they worked, and she remembered him talking about it at staff meetings there.

Afterward Peter wanted to know all about Lori's work, and he listened avidly. When she finished, he looked at Jordan, who stood behind Lori and had pretty much stayed in the background, letting the two talk without interruption, enjoying their enthusiasm over each other's projects. "It sounds so much like she's onto something really worthwhile, Jordan. What's the latest word about the grant?"

"You know how these things are," Jordan said, and then he was pointing out something to Lori, changing the subject. Something nagged at her, and she almost asked him if he'd gotten any word about it, but the two men were talking and the moment passed. If he had heard anything, she told herself, he'd have told her, whether it was good or bad. Jordan had always been honest with her. Last night he'd thought of her before himself, not taking advantage of her as other men might have been tempted to, not wanting to make love with her until she was as committed to their having a relationship as he was.

Back on the boat, she caught Jordan by surprise when she wrapped her arms around him as he started up the engine.

"What's the hug for?"

"For that incredible, perfectly marvelous surprise!" she told him, squeezing him tight.

"I'm glad you enjoyed it," he told her, his arms going around her and returning the hug. "I'd like you to see the place I worked at before I came to Aqua Vista, but it's a pretty good distance from here, and besides, I thought you'd enjoy seeing Peter's place more."

They spent the rest of the day in a leisurely fashion, sailing in and around the islands. Once Jordan encouraged Lori to take the wheel and, confident of her ability, napped in the shade of an awning he rigged up on deck. Just as she saw him awakening, she couldn't resist shutting off the engines and muttering in a panicked tone, "Oh, golly, what have I done now?"

Jordan snapped to attention, rising up to come to her side. "What is it?" he asked, running a hand through sleep-tousled hair. Then he realized that she was chuckling. "Why, you little tease! I think I'll make you walk the gangplank for waking the captain of this boat up like that!" he bellowed, advancing upon her with a threatening look.

Shrieking and laughing, she ran from him, but he caught her before she'd gone several yards. He swung her up easily into his arms, held her over the side, threatening to drop her overboard.

"I thought you said I'd have to walk the gang-plank!" she gasped, trying to catch her breath, not really afraid he'd drop her.

"Forgot I didn't have one," he told her, grinning. "I thought this was a good alternative. Convince me I shouldn't throw an impudent wench like you to the sharks!"

"Please don't!" she implored.

"Maybe if you gave me a kiss."

Lori grimaced, folded her arms over her chest and closed her eyes. "Consign me to the deep, then. Any punishment's better than kissing Captain Bligh! Ooooh!" she cried as he pretended to drop her. "Okay, okay, one kiss!"

He brought her back over the side, and his mouth came down on hers, his kiss hard and compelling. Lori put her arms around his neck and lost herself in kissing him, giving as she was getting. "Mmm," she said when she drew back. "I think that's one punishment I could get to like!"

"Okay, what else have you done to deserve punish-ment?"

"Hmm." She tried to think. "Listen, I'm willing to take on cooking chores, since you're doing the sailing. But next time you decide to go acting the pirate, you'd better lay in more provisions. Namely, *food*. I'm hungry, and your galley's pretty bare. Must be the sea air."

"Then I guess that's the first order of business," he

said, sighing, setting her on her feet. "Since there's not much daylight left."

They went ashore at the next island and found a small grocery store, where they bought as much food as they could carry back. There was a shelf of island souvenirs, a pelican and an alligator and a surfer made of different shells, and plastic rolling eyes that caught Lori's eye. She nudged Jordan and directed his attention to them, rolling her own eyes and biting her lips, attempting to hold back her mirth.

"Aren't they sweet? My sister makes them," said the shopkeeper, coming to stand beside them.

Lori's giggle caught in her throat at the sound of the woman's voice. She coughed. "Er, yes, we were just admiring them. Jordan was just saying he couldn't decide which one he liked best."

Jordan shot her a look that was meant to wither but only caused Lori to bite her lips again. "Since it's for you, sweetheart," he emphasized the endearment meaningfully, "I think the poodle, don't you?"

Beaming, the woman went to ring up one poodle at $14.95, adding it to their other purchases. "You think you've had the last laugh, don't you?" Lori asked him over the bag she carried in her arms. "*I'm* not the one out $14.95."

"I know. And I'm not the one who'll get to proudly display it, either."

She glared at him, and then they were laughing as they returned to the boat. They put the groceries away in the galley, Jordan first placing the poodle atop the refrigerator, so that every time Lori went to place something inside it she erupted into a fresh gale of giggles.

And then Jordan was picking her up, carrying her to his bed, and the giggles stopped. "We've been plundering," he said in a husky voice. "Now I'm in the mood for a long sea voyage, aren't you?"

"Seen through the porthole?" she asked impudently, and then all merriment faded from her voice and her face as she said seriously, "I'd like nothing better than to see the morning sun and the evening stars through the porthole with you."

And then there was no sound but the gentle lapping of the waves against the hull, no sight seen but each other's face and body as they made love.

A ribbon of highway bound the limestone and coral-based stepping-stones called the Keys together, part of it built upon remains of "Flagler's Folly," the railroad that the hotel and rail tycoon of the early 1900s had hoped would join the islands to each other and to the mainland. But Jordan and Lori traveled the islands in a different way on his boat, building on the awareness that had sprung up between them from their first meeting at the facility and growing as the hours passed on their lazy journey in the sun. Lori found herself wondering if they would find something more solid was being formed from the past and the present that might be a bridge to the future.

Exploring the remains of sunken Spanish galleons off an island in scuba gear the next morning led to exploring each other's personal histories as they rested after eating lunch.

Lori found herself telling Jordan what she'd never told anyone, except Joe and Polly, about what it had been like to live for several years in the orphanage to which she'd been sent after her parents were killed when she was five. She waited for the inevitable sympathy and thanked him silently when he didn't offer it. Like the pity that served no purpose for the children with whom she had worked, Lori neither needed nor wanted useless sympathy, and Jordan sensed it. At least she'd had Joe and Polly to wipe away the memory of the loneliness, the feeling of being all alone in the world; some of the other children at the orphanage had never had that. Jordan listened to her tell him how she'd withdrawn into herself at first, until the staff had begun to wonder if she was suffering from something worse than grief. "As if there were something worse than losing the ones you love," she mused, shaking her head at the memory. "They were just so short of staff that no one really had time to sit down and figure out what was wrong. Anyway, they did tests and found out I was okay, and eventually I adjusted, as everyone does."

"So that's why the empathy with the children in your project," he said softly. "They're locked within themselves too, in a way, just as you were within yourself." He reached out and took her hand in his.

Startled for a moment by his perception, she said, "I guess that's it."

"So tell me about your foster parents."

Lori smiled. All memories of them were pleasant. "One day the kids were treated to a day at Aqua World, a marine park a few miles away. What a place it was! I'd never in my life seen anything like it."

She told him how she'd walked around, enchanted, gazing starry-eyed at the stars that were moving animals at the bottom of the man-made tidal pool, utterly entranced at the sight of dolphins leaping and performing for their trainers.

"But then there was Billy," she told him, wrinkling her nose. "He was this awful boy who was always bullying me, to the point that Miss Bushner, one of the orphanage staff, insisted that I had to stop playing victim to his tauntings and mistreatment. Only nothing I did ever worked. He followed me all over the place, picking at me and tormenting me. Finally, as if he hadn't done enough, he stole my dollar, the one each of us had been given to buy something at the park gift shop.

"I knew Miss Bushner wouldn't give me another dollar, and it just about broke my heart that I couldn't buy this little plastic dolphin. So for the first time in my life I stole something, and naturally, Billy saw and told on me. Miss Bushner was hollering at me when Joe happened by. He came in to see what all the ruckus was about. He scared me half to death, this great big man with huge hands and a long, bristly gray mustache he kept curled up at the ends. He was dressed in the captain's hat and blue blazer he wore for the dolphin shows, only I thought it was a policeman's uniform. I knew people went to jail for shoplifting, even if I *didn't* know kids weren't sent there. I was absolutely terrified, and I ran out of the shop and hid."

Jordan listened to how Joe had found Lori sitting on the ledge of one of the dolphin tanks, crying over one of the dolphins, who was resting her head in her lap. Instead of hauling Lori off to jail, as she'd expected, Joe had given her the little plastic dolphin she'd wanted so badly.

"And so much more." She traced the lines on the

inside of Jordan's palm with one finger. "For my 'punishment,' I had to go to Aqua World every day after school on my bike and help feed the dolphins. There were supposed to be other chores too, but somehow they never materialized. Joe just let me sit and be with the dolphins, feed them, play with them, talk with them. And one day not long after that, I went to live there with him and his wife, Polly. She was a sweet, quiet sort of woman who was a perfect balance for Joe's outgoing personality. Because I was so fascinated by the park and the sea, I was closer to him than her. Polly stayed at home and provided the warmth there we both needed. She died of a heart attack when I was sixteen; Joe, several years later."

"They sounded nice," Jordan remarked.

"They were, but those poor people." She shook her head and smiled wryly. "I wonder if they knew what they were getting into. Maybe they wouldn't have talked the authorities into letting me come to live with them as a foster child. Joe and Polly were considered too old to adopt me, but I was left indefinitely with them as a foster kid after they took the matter to a court. And then they found out what trouble really was. At first I wanted to be good so I'd be allowed to stay. But subconsciously I needed to test his love, and I behaved so badly they should have sent me right back." She paused and laughed, then shook her head ruefully. "*I'd* have sent me back. I don't know how they stood me. What did they need with another mouth to feed—with all the animals and dolphins at Aqua World, I mean, when it wasn't doing too well financially. But I was never sent back, no matter how I provoked them; I learned that love meant being loved for myself, not for my ability to be something that I thought someone else wanted."

"It sounds like they taught you a pretty valuable lesson," Jordan said quietly.

"Yes," she agreed with a smile. She gazed around her. The sun was shining, the day was balmy, not too hot, because of the trade winds, and they were the only two people on the island. Although she hadn't wanted to come away with him at first, now she knew there was nowhere else she wanted to be other than here, with him.

"Teach me a lesson," she asked playfully, trailing her finger up his wrist, his bare arm, over his chest to a male nipple visible through a tangle of dark hair.

"Lori, about loving someone for themselves . . ." Jordan began, then as her fingers began circling the sensitive skin, he broke off, obviously having trouble concentrating.

She leaned forward to touch her tongue to the place her fingers had lightly caressed and discovered a man—this man at least!—reacted much as she did when someone touched her breast.

He caught at her hands, arresting their movement. "Stop that, Lori, please. I've been wanting to talk to you."

Her lips left his chest and moved up his strong neck to wander over his mouth. He tried not to respond, he really did, but he lasted about two seconds, to her count. Then he was falling backward to the sand, taking her with him in his arms.

Lying atop him, she gazed down into his eyes. "We can talk later. Teach me what pleases you."

"*You* do," he said.

"But what specifically?" She stroked the hair on his chest that led, like a curling black arrow, down into the waistband of his swimming briefs. "This?"

"Yes," he moaned.

"And this?" Feeling daring, she slipped her hand inside, touched him, caressed him, found his response thrilling.

For an answer, he was flipping her onto her back, removing the scraps of material that she wore for swimwear and stripping off his own suit. "And *this*," he told her, lowering himself into her innermost depths.

And then there was no more talking as they moved in instinctive motions that needed no lessons. Neither was the master; both found new ways to excite and please the other. Lori felt the aching tension build in her, build in her until she trembled on the verge of ecstasy. She stroked his back with her hands and the thrusts of his body increased in tempo and the expression of love in his eyes pierced her very soul.

She felt the tension expand and then snap, like a bubble of air that reached the surface. A warm sea of pleasure washed over her, its momentum increased a few moments later when Jordan shuddered in her arms and turned his face into her neck. Lori held him, treasuring the closeness of the moment.

8

~~~~~~~~~~~~~~~~

After a time they got up to wade into the sea. They cupped water in their hands and let it run over each other's bodies, laughing as the waves pushed them together intimately, and then they weren't laughing any more. They stared at each other, smiles fading. Jordan took her hand and led her out of the water, and they lay on the sand and made love again.

Only when the sun began setting in a spectacular display and the sand grew cool did they climb back aboard the boat and seek another place for their pleasure.

The next time they went into the sea the following afternoon, they wore their swimsuits and scuba gear. Gliding beneath the surface, holding hands with Jordan, Lori thought she'd never been so enthralled with the beauty of the underwater world, all her senses sharpened by the lovemaking they'd shared that morning.

Underwater "flowers" that were often animal as well as plant bloomed beneath them: daisylike animals called anemones, bright masses of hot pink and crimson-colored coral, sea urchins that looked like puffy chrysanthemums.

Crayfish formed a social group beside a clump of seaweed, gesturing with their claws and antennae—A gossip party? Lori wondered fancifully. A school of fish swam toward them, a shifting kaleidoscope of brilliant colors—scarlet, purple, chartreuse—and shapes—shiny round scales on bodies that were oblong or triangular or tubelike. The school divided and deflected, passed at each side and reformed a few feet away from them. A sea turtle swam by, his gliding movements less cumbersome in the buoyancy of the water than those of his land counterpart.

Jordan found a piece of rose-colored coral that had been broken off either by an inhabitant of the sea or the motion of the water itself. Although coral hardened on contact with air, the organism was fragile. Because people had endangered the coral by tearing off clumps of it for souvenirs or for sale, this barrier reef that lay along the coastline of Florida was now protected by law.

They separated to swim around the broken hull of another old ship that had foundered and sunk in these waters, but found no treasure. A large grouper fish, one of the sea's uglier inhabitants with its muddy colors and bulbous lips, peered at them from within a hole punctured in the side of the ship. The fish pursed its lips, as if in annoyance at their intrusion, and disappeared from sight.

Lori found the wood of the ship soggy beneath her fingers; then Jordan was touching her shoulder. He'd found a triton on the floor of the sea, a spiral, trumpet-shaped shell of browns and white with a pearly white lip, bigger than two of Jordan's hands.

Knowing she collected shells—she had found several really special ones on the island yesterday to take back home—he handed it to her.

Lori thanked him silently with her eyes for his gift from the sea, and something wordless passed between them. They moved together to embrace, removing their regulators, forsaking the air in their tanks for a kiss that became a rapture of the deep from which they did not want to emerge.

At last they did, fitting the regulators to their mouths. They swam again for a time, exchanging glances now and then that said both weren't really all that conscious of the beauty around them anymore, too aware of each other to see much else. Finally, by unspoken agreement, they swam back to the boat.

"C'mon, mermaid, I'm starved even if you don't get hungry," said Jordan, helping her off with her equipment.

"That's why you rushed me back here?" she pretended to complain, knowing the real reason for his eagerness.

They raided the refrigerator and cupboards in the galley. Sitting cross-legged on the deck, they ate the various things they'd found: a can of deviled ham spread on crackers, eaten with chunks of sharp cheddar and sweet pickles. Lori had never cared for deviled ham—actually, it was a little spicy for her stomach—but she really didn't care what she ate. She wondered if it was the salt air heightening her appetite —or just pure unadulterated happiness. "Mmm, this is good," she murmured, licking her fingers as she ate one of the mangoes they'd picked on the island yesterday and carried back to the boat. "They're good, but awfully juicy." She wiped at her chin with her hand and grimaced at the stickiness. "Thank goodness no one's around to see me being a messy eater."

"This is the only way to eat a mango, with your fingers," he told her as he finished his.

"No, the fingers should be eaten separately," she deadpanned, quoting the famous etiquette expert when asked if fried chicken should be eaten with the fingers.

"You should be glad Aphrodite isn't here, or she'd be carrying on the way she did when I made that bad pun around her!" He dropped the peel to his plate and reached for one of her juice-stained hands. He licked the juice from her fingers one by one, the gesture and the movement of his tongue made even more erotic by the way he looked steadily at her, watching her reaction. He continued with her other hand, and then he pulled her closer and licked at the juice on her chin. Her lips were next as his tongue moved over them, too, tasting the juice on their parted softness and finally dipping inside.

They savored the ripe tropical fruit on each other's tongues, hot and sweet, and Lori's senses swam as the kiss went deeper, became more passionate. His hand touched her breast, the touch electric through the thin fabric of the bikini top. He broke the kiss to move the top aside, kissing her breast. Lori lifted his hand to her lips and repeated the caress he'd performed on her palm, licking the warm sticky juice from his fingers. She admired their long, well-formed shape. She tongued a circle on his palm and felt her desire grow as he closed his eyes and groaned.

He kissed her lips again, and his hand slid inside the other cup of the bikini top. His palm wet with her own saliva was unbearably erotic as he cupped her breast, his thumb gently caressing its tip as it hardened. He pulled at the string that held the top together, and it fell away.

Apparently fascinated by the easy access, he kissed both breasts, and she clutched at his hair, conscious only of the heat rising in her body. His hand slid down to rest, heavy and warm, upon the small triangle of fabric that formed the bottom of the bikini, which barely covered her, before suddenly surprising her by slipping inside it, exploring her intimately as they kissed. Soon, as if tired of the restricted space the snugly tied bikini allowed, he raised himself on one side and untied it, his expression hungry as he gazed on her.

"Every time I see you, you seem to be dressed in this color of aqua," he mused. "That's how I knew it must be your favorite."

Instead of removing the scrap of fabric when she raised her hips slightly to help him, he spread the top triangle of the bikini bottom down over the deck between her legs. "But I think I like you in *this* color best."

He kissed her bare tanned stomach, and her eyes closed in ecstasy. His kisses trailed lower, and he pressed them where his fingers had been. Her eyes flew open at the unexpected and astonishingly powerful reaction to the intimacy. Heat grew and grew until it felt as if the sun had suddenly lowered in the sky and she was glowing with the intensity of its rays where Jordan knelt between her legs. Stars burst behind her closed eyelids, silver and red and blue, then she felt herself become as light and free as the clouds overhead. Finally she floated down to earth to find herself cradled in Jordan's arms, heard waves lapping against the boat, felt it rocking gently beneath them.

"You okay?" he murmured, nuzzling his lips against her temple, pushing her wet hair back from her face.

"Marvelous," she said, smiling at him dreamily.

"There's that smile, the one that reminds me of Aphrodite's. I'd think being made love to made you smile that way if I didn't know better. You wore it before you ever had," he explained when she didn't appear to understand his words. He was silent for a moment. "Why me, Lori? There must have been other men you were attracted to through the years."

Not the way I was to you, she thought, but she didn't say the words aloud, because she really didn't know why she'd been drawn to him enough to make the first move. Why she'd wanted him, and wanted much more with him. "I don't know," she said finally. "Once I wanted to make love with a man, not long after Joe died. Then I realized we didn't want the same thing. I was vulnerable, suddenly without a parent figure. I wanted love, and he wanted merely sexual gratification."

She raised up. "Anyway, I don't really want to talk about anyone else when I'm with you. I can think of lots better things to do, can't you?"

His black eyes were impenetrable as he studied her, but a smile tugged at the corners of his mouth. "Like what?"

"Like have you teach me how to make you feel as wonderful as I did a moment ago," she whispered, and heard his swift intake of breath.

"You don't have—"

Lori placed her fingers on his mouth. "Did you like doing that for me?"

"More than you did having me love you."

She kissed his chest. "Then I'm going to love making love to you too. Let me?" The last wasn't a statement but a question, and he heard it, for he was nodding slowly.

She kissed all the places she had learned excited him, and a few more she discovered. His skin tasted of salt from the sea, and she felt the tightening and shifting of his muscles beneath her lips. After the strength in those muscles she'd seen as he swam, that she'd felt against her hands whenever they touched, she was unprepared for how he trembled beneath the caresses of lips and hands.

His breathing became shallow, his heartbeat erratic, and she knew it was hard for him to let her stroke the heat in him when he'd already been aroused before she'd begun.

Once she looked up to see him staring at her with

eyes that glittered beneath heavy lids, his expression one of surprised pleasure. His hands brushed at the tumbled mass of her hair and they smiled at each other, and then she wiped the smile from his mouth as she gave him the ecstasy he had given her, and more. She heard her name and some words said as a groan was wrenched out of him and he shook with spasms of love that seemed almost painful for him.

Moving up to lie in his arms, Lori listened to the sound of his breathing and his heartbeat, aware of a sense of wonder at how her loving had taken him to such heights. He looked . . . dazzled, and she knew it wasn't because of the sun that had been in his eyes. "There are no words for how you made me feel," he whispered.

Lori turned her face up to his. The look they had exchanged beneath the sea only a short time ago returned, triggering a tide of emotion within her that threatened to swamp her composure, which was already shaken by what had happened between them.

Jordan's heartbeats returned to normal, his breathing rate slowed and after a time she knew that he slept.

Far from relaxing after their lovemaking, though, Lori's mind and body were restless. The more she tried to close her eyes and take a short nap, as Jordan was doing, the more she just couldn't settle.

Rising quietly, she pulled on her bikini and went to stand at the bow, gazing out at the sea sparkling in the late afternoon sunlight. Whenever she felt confused about something or needed to think, what she found helpful was a swim. Being in the water always soothed her, gave her peace. But Jordan was asleep. Still, she knew he'd wake soon. She'd noticed he had the ability to nap briefly and wake up without any need for an alarm. If anyone had told me two days ago I'd know things like that about this man, that I'd be here on his boat like this, making love with him, I'd have told them they were crazy, thought Lori with a smile.

Lori hugged herself. She knew what was bothering her. Her feelings for Jordan were running so deep so quickly, they confused and frightened her. Especially when she didn't know how he felt. Occasionally she'd catch him looking at her, an unreadable expression in his eyes, but he'd said nothing of his feelings. This had started out as a weekend away—now what was happening? Was she falling in love with him? There had been such gaps in being loved—in loving—in her life. Since Joe had followed Polly and her parents into death, she hadn't known that kind of love for a long time. She knew loneliness had no clock, no sense of reason—but she had felt alone again for a long time, isolated in spite of having friends like Betsy and Mrs. Yamamoto.

And she'd never experienced a man's love for a woman, or a woman's for a man. She'd never dated much, and her one serious relationship with a man, Robert, hadn't worked out. She'd begun to think she'd go through life alone. Like the solitary island-dweller unexpectedly confronted with a companion after resigning himself to a life without another human, Lori's discovery of feelings, of just a growing caring for him, troubled her. Was this love or just infatuation?

Pacing the deck didn't calm her, didn't diminish her nervous energy. The water was so calm, and she'd never had any problems diving. She told herself it couldn't hurt to go diving alone for the few minutes before Jordan woke and joined her. After pulling on her equipment, she slipped into the water, hoping the splash wouldn't wake him.

She swam, trying to sort out her emotions. The cramp in her stomach was so sudden and fierce it took her breath away, doubled her. A burst of air bubbles floated upward at her distress.

Fighting to calm herself, Lori took a deep breath and rubbed at her stomach. She was hurting so badly that she couldn't tell if she'd gone down too soon after eating or if her ulcer was flaring up at the food she'd ingested. I shouldn't have eaten that deviled ham, thought Lori.

Another cramp seized her, and she drew into a fetal ball, clutching at her middle. This was why divers were always told to dive with a buddy. She'd known it before she'd come down, only now was too late to go telling herself how stupid she'd been. Now she just had to get up to the boat somehow.

The activity of underwater creatures around her had lessened, she noticed between cramps. At first she thought she'd been the cause of their scurrying into the protective cover of aquatic plants, rocks, anywhere they could hide. She became aware that she was being watched, that she wasn't alone. Not that she had been before, with hundreds of pairs of eyes upon her from countless fishes and other sea life.

But this was different.

A shadow fell over her and she glanced up, thought with relief, Jordan's coming!

And then her heartbeats tripped as she realized the dark looming shape wasn't Jordan but the predator she'd at first compared him to—a shark!

Fascinated, as always, as it passed eerily nearby, Lori watched the feared predator. The shark was nearly as long as she was tall, swimming slowly and sinuously as it circled her. She tried to stay still but occasionally a cramp seized her and made her move slightly, made a burst of air bubbles float upward in the water. She was cautious, careful, more respectful than fearful of the shark. After all, she knew it was dangerous only if it confused her for a wounded fish. If she stayed as she was, she'd be left alone. She hoped.

Lori gazed through her mask at the shadow of the boat above and off slightly to her right, wishing she could somehow communicate telepathically with Jordan and he'd come to help. Then she banished that thought, afraid he might and that *he'd* get hurt.

But despite all she'd done not to attract its attention, not to betray her vulnerability, the shark moved in for a closer look. Teeth bared in a predatory snarl, it brushed close enough for Lori to see its unblinking eye fixed upon her. Near enough for Lori to see the bits of flesh clinging to its teeth, remnants of its last meal. The gun-metal gray body moved past, and she breathed a sigh of relief at seeing the back of its tail fin. But she knew it might return.

As if it scented her fear in the water or somehow read her thoughts, the shark returned to circle her.

Waiting to see what would happen next, crouched down, even the terrible pains in her stomach forgotten as a bigger problem loomed supreme, Lori couldn't help wishing for the presence of Aphrodite or any other dolphin right then. They had occasionally come to the aid of swimmers or divers through the ages; often just their being in the water beside a human was enough to discourage an attack by a shark. Sometimes dolphins offered a fin or their back to help the human to safety. And sometimes, when it became necessary, they took on this master of the sea domain, at great speed ramming their head into the side of the shark, killing it if necessary.

The strangest thought hit her then: Jordan was probably getting sunburned up there because he had probably not awakened yet, and she wasn't there to rouse him. And might never be. Then she was mentally shaking her head at the twilight zone her mind had wandered into. Was she getting hysterical, she who knew if she stayed calm she'd probably be all right? Surely she wasn't one of those people infected with the mania about "Jaws."

Lori didn't know what it was, instinct perhaps, but something told her that when the shark came at her this time, it was for an attack. What she knew about warding off a shark flashed into her mind. *Ram it, hit it hard as you can between its eyes, where it's vulnerable, and you'll probably frighten it away. It's not used to its prey fighting back. Just stay calm; don't panic and you'll be all right and laughing about this on deck with Jordan in a few minutes.*

The shark lunged at her and as its jaws opened and she caught a glimpse of long, deadly teeth, Lori brought her fist down fast and hard between its eyes, a shark's most vulnerable place.

Her aim was good; the shark's jaws snapped shut, and it jerked convulsively. The powerful movement sent a wide swath of water against her, throwing her off balance, stirred up a blinding rush of sand so that she couldn't see for paralyzing moments.

Then it was settling, and as she gazed upward warily, the light was blocked out by another shadow. This time the shadow was Jordan, and her relief was so great that unthinkingly she straightened and pushed herself up off the sandy bottom of the sea. The sudden movement sent an excruciating flash of pain through her stomach, and she writhed in the water, sending up a spray of air bubbles.

She felt his arms go around her, and he brought his face close to hers, peering at her with fearful eyes. He pulled at her hands, which clutched her stomach, and appeared relieved when he saw she had no injury. He helped her swim slowly to the surface, pausing now and then for a cramp to run its course, always alert for the return of the shark.

Finally they reached the boat and climbed aboard. After Jordan's concern for her below, it came as a shock when Lori was pushed almost roughly ahead of him. He hauled himself up next and began taking off his diving equipment, almost tearing the straps and tanks from his body.

"You stupid, crazy fool!" he shouted. "You violated the first rule of diving that everyone's taught in the first five minutes of scuba lessons. You *know* you're never supposed to dive alone, *never*, because of the very possibility of what just happened!"

Lori listened to him rant, astonished. Her hands fumbled, stilled on her straps. "But I knew you'd be joining me!" she protested.

"Oh, did you? What if I hadn't?" he stormed, furious. "What if I had overslept? Then what? Look at this, Lori, you'd nearly used up your air even if the shark hadn't gotten you."

She knew in her distress she'd used more air, but she said, "The air was no problem. Back when I dove for oysters in the Japanese pearl lagoon at Aqua World, I could go without air longer than any of the other girls. I'd have just spaced my air out—"

"For crissake, don't feed me that tourist crap about pearl divers at a time like this, will you?" He grasped her shoulders, his fingers biting into them. "Damn it, Lori, what about the shark? I suppose you're going to tell me that was nothing too?"

"Well, you're acting like he was Jaws himself," she said, trying to reason with him. But her words sounded hollow, lacking in defense even to her. "It was just a small reef shark, and it left after I hit him on the head. You've been a diver for years; you know they're not that dangerous!"

He threw up his hands, shaking his head. "God, Lori, if you knew what it did to me, seeing that shark going at you while I was too far away to do anything! And then you sit there calmly telling me you just hit him on the head and he went away and everything's all right. . . ." He stopped, as if talking about it was only making it worse. He clutched her, held her so tightly she couldn't breathe. She slipped her arms around his waist and let him hold her, needing to be close too. And then he was blindly seeking her mouth with his, pressing it down savagely on hers, forcing her lips apart, his tongue ravaging the interior of her mouth.

The ferocity of his kiss shocked her more than the suddenness of it. Instinctively she struggled against its harshness and his hands hurting her shoulders. Demanding and possessive as his lovemaking had been more than once, he'd never behaved as he was now. She felt him pushing her down onto the hardness of the deck, his hands as rough on her body as his mouth was upon hers.

His hands pushed away the diving equipment from her shoulders and he pulled at her bikini, tearing it in his haste to strip it from her body. She felt suddenly vulnerable, exposed like a sea creature stripped of its protective shell. "Jordan, please, stop!" she cried.

But Jordan was yanking off his own suit, dragging the wet garment that clung like a second skin down and off his hips and legs, baring his body. The aroused physical power of his maleness hadn't frightened her before, but now it did.

Lori lifted her eyes to his and what she saw in his expression calmed her. On Jordan's face was fear and desperation mingled with a passion to make intimate contact with her so that he'd really believe she was safe, she realized. More than her skin was touched by what was driving him; she felt something stir deep inside her, deeper than her own vulnerability and fear. She saw that he had been terrified for her, terrified, whether it was reasonable or not to be. He cared for her too, she saw, more than he'd ever let on, cared deeply. He needed reassurance that he hadn't lost her, that she was safe here with him.

And now she knew his fear, understood it because it hit her then—hit her far harder than it had for a moment below—what could have happened. She could have lost *him* by never seeing him again, and he was suddenly more important than life itself to her.

He caught her up in his frenzy, carrying her along on a rising wave of desire, of intense passion. Their kisses and caresses were wild and primitive. Part of him was probing, hard and hot and insistent, against her. She brought him inside her warmth, meeting and matching his rhythm with her own. There was no longer any need or desire for him to be gentle; she didn't want him to be. What was happening was too powerful, too elemental, too basic, for either of them to contain it or subdue it or express it any other way.

Instead of minding the heaviness of his body pressing her against the unyielding hard deck or the brush of his hands on the scraped patches on her skin that sent not-so-pleasant tingles along her nerves, Lori reveled in all of it, exhilarated even, because experiencing the pain as well as the pleasure of ecstasy meant she was alive and she was here with him.

They surged together, rose higher and higher in the storm, a hurricane that swept them up, up, past the peaks they'd reached before; finally they were cast adrift in mindless release, collapsing against each other.

In the silence that lingered after the storm, Jordan lay spent, his lips against her neck. Lori held him, arms wrapped around his back, until at last he shifted to his side, saying, "I'm too heavy for you."

She shook her head but said nothing, overwhelmed.

He passed a hand over his face. "I never meant that to happen, Lori," he said with a ragged moan as he gazed at her, looking troubled. "I hurt you, didn't I? God, it wasn't enough what you went through; then I had to yell at you and then practically attack you."

"Stop it!" she whispered, reaching up to touch his

cheek. "I'm all right, or I will be, if you just hold me. And, Jordan?"

He raised up on one elbow to stare down at her. "Yes?"

"My cramps are gone," she said with a smile.

"Oh, Lori," he said. "What am I going to do with you?" He picked her up and carried her below to the shower. Tenderly he washed and toweled her and treated her where the brush of the shark's sharp skin had abraded her legs. And then he climbed into bed with her and held her in his arms.

9

~~~~~~~~~~~~~~~

Stabbing pains in her stomach woke Lori. Not wanting to disturb Jordan, she got up and padded on bare feet into the galley, taking her purse and the caftan from atop the dresser with her.

Finding the prescription bottle inside the purse by a small light over the sink, she was dismayed to find that she had only one capsule left. Debating whether she should take it or keep it in case the pain got worse, Lori finally swallowed it with a glass of water. She slipped on the caftan, snapped off the light and climbed the stairs to the deck above. She sat down, wrapping her arms around her knees, which she had drawn up to her chest.

There were miles and miles of nothing but sea around her, the tips of the waves edged with silver beneath the light of a sliver of a moon. She felt lonely, but it had nothing to do with the fact that she was sitting here alone. Even in a crowd she sometimes felt that way. Knowing a lot of her lonely feeling came from the child who had never stopped hoping parents would show up to say it had all been a mistake, they were alive, Lori forced her thoughts on a more adult plane. But that only brought up the earlier turmoil she'd been feeling about what was happening between herself and Jordan.

"Lori? What's the matter?"

She turned and strained to see him in the darkness. "Nothing, I just can't sleep." Her words reminded her of how she hadn't been able to sleep the other night and how she'd come up here to make love with Jordan.

"Is it because of this afternoon?" he asked as he carefully found his way over to her, sat down beside her and peered, concerned, into her face. "Are you afraid of having bad dreams?"

"Jordan, I didn't encounter Jaws," she told him with a wry smile.

"That's a matter of opinion," he growled. He was silent for a moment. "Is it because of the way I behaved? I'm sorry, Lori, I—"

"That's not it," she cut in quickly. Well, it's part of it, thought Lori. But not the way you think. A spasm of pain crossed her face, and even though she averted her face and it was dark, he saw it.

"It's your stomach, isn't it? Why didn't you wake me and tell me you were in pain?"

Shrugging, Lori rested her chin on her knees. "Why keep two people awake?"

"Because I care about you, Lori. Is there anything I can do for you? Did you take your medication? Oh, my God," he said, in the midst of his rapid-fire questions. "Tell me you had it in your purse when I hauled you on this boat."

"I had it," she reassured him.

He subsided, although she could see he was still worried. "You took it and it didn't do any good?"

"Sometimes it takes awhile."

"But it will, *eventually?*"

"Sometimes I just have to wait it out," she admitted.

"Does it feel worse than usual tonight? Those were pretty bad cramps you were having in the water this afternoon. Maybe it's something more this time. I've heard ulcers can bleed, maybe I should get you to a hospital."

"*Jordan!* I'll be all right!"

"Then what do we do?"

"*I* wait it out. You go back to sleep. There's nothing you can do. But thanks," she added.

"Lori, I care about you. I want to be with you and help in any way I can. Unless you don't want me to, unless I'm really part of what's making you hurt."

She didn't want him to know how close he'd been to the truth, and so she said, "Jordan, ulcers aren't just caused by emotions; they usually have a physical origin, you know."

He didn't look convinced. "Then will it help if I just hold you and we talk?"

That was the last thing she needed right now, to have his arms around her, to have to sit and talk normally with him when her emotions were still in as much of an uproar as her stomach. "Jordan, maybe we should start back home. I—didn't want to tell you, but I took my last pill and I might need more."

"Why didn't you say so?"

"Don't be angry with me."

He touched her cheek. "Hey, I'm not. I'm just a little . . . exasperated that you didn't want to let me try to help you. Look, we're not that far from home now; I've been retracing our route here to get us back tomorrow anyway. We'll just start back tonight." He hugged her, kissed her forehead and got up. "Why don't you go crawl back into bed and try to get some sleep? I'll wake you when we get there."

Lori knew she wouldn't get any sleep, but at least there she wouldn't have to act as if nothing other than her stomach was bothering her. "Okay," she said, and she went to do as he suggested.

She must have dozed, because what felt like no time later, he was shaking her shoulder gently to wake her. "Lori? We're back at the marina. I'm going to telephone the drugstore and get you a refill."

"You don't have to do that," she told him, sitting up in bed. "I have some more at my apartment."

"I'll go get them."

"I'd really feel better there, if you don't mind. Sometimes the motion of a boat makes me worse," she lied. Anything, just to get away, to be alone and have a chance to think things through.

If he thought her eager to be away from him, he didn't seem to notice. "Sure, get dressed and I'll drive you home."

At the door it was another matter entirely. "I'd like to stay and make sure you're better," he insisted when she told him she'd be fine.

"I'm much better already," she argued. "Please, Jordan, I just want to go to sleep again and I . . . won't do that with you here."

"I promise to behave."

"Just promise me you won't let me eat any more deviled ham," she said lightly.

"I'll stock whatever you can eat next time I 'kidnap' you," he teased in return, his words reminding her how unwilling she had been to go along.

"I had a lovely time," she told him a little formally, not sure what to do next. She'd never been in the position of saying good-bye to a lover before.

But Jordan was easing the awkwardness, taking matters into his own hands—or rather arms, pulling her to him for a kiss. "This isn't the end of us, Lori, it's a beginning. I promise." Then he was gone.

Her sleep was restless, filled with dreams she'd been too exhausted to have on the boat coming back. A shark pursued her through them, changing into Jordan before her eyes, then changing back again. Lori got up, showered and dressed. Her pills had worked, and she realized she was starved. She went to eat a late lunch at The Sea Dragon and was disappointed to be told by the waitress on duty that her friends, the Yamamotos, had taken the day off to see their grand-children.

Passing the facility on the way home, Lori thought about stopping by to see how Aphrodite was doing but was afraid she'd run into Jordan. She decided to call Betsy later to ask her about the dolphin.

Although the day was overcast, she went for a walk on the beach behind her apartment house. Vague plans for the remaining days of her vacation filtered through her mind, but she couldn't concentrate on them, and that bothered her. She liked to have a clear-cut purpose in her personal life as well as professional life, and in both she felt she was just drifting with the tide at the moment.

A storm was brewing far offshore. Eerie flashes of lightning lit the sky miles out over the sea. Goose bumps rose on her skin as a brisk wind whipped whitecaps atop the waves and blew bits of foam at Lori's feet as she walked close to the shoreline.

Joe had told her the foam was mermaids' bubbles, the first day she'd come to live with him, she remembered with an inward smile. She'd never liked swimming in the heavily chlorinated pool at the Y the orphanage kids visited in the summer, but she took to the sea "like a fish" as Polly put it, developing an insatiable curiosity about everything in it, which they encouraged. Joe had a way of mixing truth and myth about the sea, challenging her to know the difference, as in the fiction of the foam being mermaids' bubbles. Along with memories like this always came the question, Why do the people you love have to leave?

Only when the sky darkened and the wind grew cool did Lori realize how long she'd been walking. Heading back in the direction she'd come, Lori saw a man striding toward her. Although she was still some distance away, she instinctively knew that it was

Jordan. Checking an impulse to run in the opposite direction, she slowed her steps, delaying their meeting.

"You know," he remarked with a smile as they drew close, "lately I feel like I spend half my time running around looking for you."

She forced a smile to her lips. "What made you think I'd be here?"

"I know how much you love the beach. Feeling better?"

She nodded. "Yes, thanks."

He took her hand, and they walked for a time without talking. Several times Jordan glanced at her, until finally he said, "Look, Lori, is something bothering you? I thought there might be on the way back. I put it down to your not feeling well but now . . ." He stopped, and she had to stop too. Tilting her chin up, he looked directly into her eyes.

"There's nothing wrong," she told him, pulling away.

He frowned. "I don't believe that." When she said nothing, he sighed. "Look, something's been bothering *me* since just before we left on the boat. I hesitated to tell you because I was . . . afraid it might keep us from enjoying each other. And then I couldn't find a way to tell you and maybe chance spoiling what I thought you were beginning to feel for me. But right now I'm a little confused. I don't know if you feel anything, and if you do, if this makes a difference . . ." He broke off to rake a hand through wind-tousled black hair. "Hell, I know what I did was wrong but—"

Lori had a premonition of what it was Jordan was having difficulty telling her. She licked her suddenly dry lips. "Why don't you just tell me what it is you did?"

He shoved his hands deep in the pockets of the white denims he wore, making the material stretch taut over his hips and thighs, almost, but not quite, distracting her from his next words.

He took a deep breath and plunged in. "Lori, I'd give you the sun and the moon and the stars if I could," he told her, his voice intense. "I've tried as hard as I can, but I can't seem to get you a grant for your work right now. I even went to Washington to talk to some people—"

"You knew before the trip?"

He expelled a breath harshly. "Yes."

"Why didn't you tell me?"

"I was afraid if I told you, you wouldn't hear anything else."

"What more was there to hear?" she retorted bitterly, feeling betrayed.

"That I love you."

"Oh, really? And since you admitted not telling me something to get what you wanted this weekend, you're probably saying you love me just so that you can get—get something."

"All I want is your love."

"That's a hell of a way to get it!" she shot back.

"I said I know I was wrong. When I said a little while ago that lately I feel like I've been spending half my time running around looking for you—the other half I've been spending wondering why you keep running from me."

"I think you've just told me why I was instinctively

doing it!" With that she turned and did what he'd said she'd been doing—ran.

"That's your answer to everything, isn't it, to run away and hide, to find reasons to be angry with me so you don't have to admit you're afraid of what you feel for me!" he called after her.

She stopped, spun around. "All I feel for you is . . . disgust, Jordan! I've always thought everyone in this world was predator or prey, and I was right! I fell prey to your lies! I'd rather be around that shark you were so afraid had hurt me than be near you again!"

"I didn't lie to you."

"No, you're right; there's a difference, isn't there? You just lied by omission, didn't you?"

"I made a mistake. Are you going to let that wreck what we have together?"

"We have exactly nothing, Jordan!" she yelled back. This time when she turned and ran all she heard was the sound of her feet on the hard-packed sand, her own pounding heartbeat and labored breathing.

The sky opened up and she was glad for the cold wet drops on her face, because she didn't want to believe she was crying over a man like that, didn't want to believe the weekend had all been a lie. The drops became a deluge, soaking her by the time she reached her apartment, but Lori threw herself on her bed without taking off her sodden clothes, too miserable to even care. Now, without the rain, she knew the wetness on her cheeks was from tears, not rain alone, but she didn't care. Drained emotionally and physically by all that had happened in the last few days, she fell asleep.

She slept through the night and most of the following morning, waking to find herself alternately hot and cold. Her head was aching and stuffy; her throat was sore. *Great, just what I need, a cold,* she thought dismally. She spent most of the day huddled in her robe on the living room sofa, watching television without really caring what was on it. Reruns of a show she'd always hated came on, one about three women who acted surprisingly stupid for being detectives. She wondered why she sat there staring at it.

"Don't do anything smart," snarled a bad guy at the plastic-looking blonde who was one of the stars.

"Don't worry, she won't!" jeered Lori, and she got up to switch off the set. "The dumb broad's never done anything smart in her life." *But you have?* her inner voice asked cynically, reminding her of what had happened between her and Jordan.

The cold kept her captive in the apartment for the next two days, making her feel restive. The only break in the monotony of taking vitamin C and drinking hot tea and going through two boxes of tissues wiping at her nose were telephone calls from Mrs. Yamamoto and Betsy. Mrs. Yamamoto had heard Lori had been in her restaurant the other day and invited her over to chat. Informed Lori had a cold, she talked with her on the telephone instead. Lori had no trouble avoiding the topic of Jordan and the weekend on the boat, because Mrs. Yamamoto didn't know about that.

Betsy, on the other hand, did, and she wanted to know everything. "So tell me about your weekend with Jordan."

"How did you know where I was?" Lori asked, evading the question.

"Are you serious? It's all over the facility how he carried you off."

Lori groaned.

"So tell Betts all the yummy details. Where'd you go, what'd you do, how's he in bed?"

"Betsy! Honestly!"

Her friend laughed. "I just had to throw that last question in. All kidding aside, did you have fun?" She waited, and then she asked, "Lori, are you still there?"

"Yes."

"Are you crying? You sound funny."

"I have a cold."

"Oh. You're sure you're not upset about something?"

"No."

"Lori, I thought you'd only been out with him a couple of times."

"We had." Lori explained how the boat trip had come about.

"Oooh, don't you just love the masterful type?" sighed Betsy. There was a pause. "You're not saying anything. Don't you?"

"Not exactly." She hesitated, and then told Betsy about the argument on the beach the other day with Jordan, skipping over what had happened during the weekend preceding it.

"Maybe he was right, Lori. How would you have felt if he'd told you before the weekend?"

Lori frowned. "You sound as if you're saying his not telling me was okay."

"I'm just telling you I understand why he did it. He—"

162

"Listen, Betsy, someone's at the door, I've got to go. Talk to you later, okay?" She put the receiver down on Betsy's surprised, "Sure, Lori, later."

There was no one at the door. She had just found herself growing irritable with Betsy, and she wasn't like that. Was it because of her cold . . . or was it because she was beginning to wonder herself if Jordan had been right not to tell her about the grant before the weekend?

No, Jordan hadn't been right. Not about anything. She didn't need him, as he'd told her he hoped she would—not him or any other man. Not that kind of man. And she wasn't afraid of what she felt for him—whatever it was she felt, she was going to stop feeling it *now*.

Wandering around the apartment, Lori wondered why it suddenly seemed so empty when it never had before. In the space of a weekend Jordan had her thinking she was going to be lonely without him. . . .

She checked her watch, found that it was after five. She'd wanted to go see Aphrodite, and since Jordan wouldn't be at the facility at this hour, now was the time. After changing into a pair of jeans and a thin cotton sweater, she let herself out of the apartment, deciding to walk to get some sunshine and fresh air.

Aphrodite's welcome was exuberant, warming Lori's heart.

"I'm glad to see you, too," Lori told her, smiling as she bent to give the dolphin a hug. "I missed you so, Aphrodite."

"Not like I've missed you."

Lori jerked her head around at the sound of

Jordan's voice. His grin was sardonic. "You came when you thought I'd be gone, didn't you?" he asked, correctly interpreting her expression of surprise.

"Of course not. I just didn't have time to come over before. I've been busy."

"Really? I just talked to Betsy, and she said you were cooped up at your apartment with a cold and— What did you say?"

"Nothing." Lori blushed as she realized Jordan had heard her mutter, "Big-mouth Betsy."

"Lori, I . . ." Jordan stopped as she stiffened when he touched her shoulder.

"What?" she asked coldly, not bothering to look at him.

"Nothing, Lori, nothing. I was hoping after you'd had a chance to think about it, you'd realize you over-reacted. I remember what you told me about your foster parents while we were on the boat, how they taught you that love meant being loved for yourself, not for your ability to *be* something you thought someone else wanted. It also means loving someone even when they can't give you anything but their love. I didn't want my not being able to give you what you wanted so badly to stand in the way of us. My love can't replace your work, but it's all I can give you. It's all anyone can or should. I . . ." He stopped. "You let me know if you change your mind, Lori."

She listened to his footsteps fade away. Aphrodite swam over. Dolphins weren't the placid, always happy creatures some people believed; they had moods too, times when they lost patience or were stubborn or whatever, but Lori had never seen Aphrodite as annoyed as she was now. The dolphin fussed and nudged Lori's knee as she sat beside the tank. Lori didn't quite understand all of it, but she got the drift of it and admonished, "Aphrodite, ladies don't talk like that."

Aphrodite uttered a sound that was the dolphin equivalent of a disgusted snort and flicked water at Lori with her nose.

"Well, if you're mad because I haven't seen you in a while . . ." Lori started to say, then stopped abruptly. She sighed. "I know, that's not it, is it?" Aphrodite wasn't a human in a dolphin suit to her—or to a lot of other people—but a being with intelligence and emotions that humans just hadn't yet understood completely. And how a human's intelligence and emotions were understood by dolphins wasn't known either. But Aphrodite did communicate in an almost mystic way that couldn't be explained, and Lori understood the message now.

"Maybe I wasn't fair to him, reacting the way I did about him not telling me about the grant," she admitted. "But why did I act that way? Aphrodite, I want love; I want to be loved so much, to love someone else! So why am I so afraid?" Jordan *had* been right about that. . . .

But Aphrodite only regarded Lori with those eloquent eyes of hers, and Lori knew the answer to her question lay within herself.

She glanced through the chain-link fence that enclosed the area, saw Jordan talking with Ben, the night watchman, at his guard shack. "I don't know if it would even do any good to apologize to Jordan until I've figured this out." Lori sighed, getting to her feet.

Her attention focused inward, Lori didn't see the

rope coiled on the concrete near the tank until it was too late. One foot turned under her and she felt herself falling, her hands clutching at air as she fell. Her head struck the edge of the tank just before she hit the water, and her cry of surprise and pain was drowned out by seawater filling her nose and mouth. Blackness enveloped her, a cold, wet, dark emptiness that made her feel curiously light and free of all pain.

10

A mouth was pressing down on hers, hard, as Lori fought her way up from the blackness. Her chest pained, lungs straining for vital air, and yet the mouth stayed on hers, kissing her, keeping her from breathing. Then warmth was flooding through her and the mouth left and the pain was easing. Her eyelids felt heavy, too heavy to lift, but she finally managed to open them. A face swam into focus, Jordan's, his black eyes growing bigger and bigger in her field of vision until they were so large she was being swallowed up in the blackness again, only this time it wasn't a darkness free of pain, the pain was growing in her chest. His mouth pressed down and the panicked thought raced through her mind, *I can't breathe, I can't breathe! Don't . . . kiss . . . Air, please!* A rush of warm breath filled her mouth, and her lungs gulped it in desperately. The mouth left hers, and she gasped, opening her eyes, staring up into Jordan's face in terror. Her breath was suspended, not coming in, not going out. His mouth joined with hers, and again he was helping her breathe, only she was just realizing that's what he'd been doing. He withdrew his mouth and was jerking his head away. She heard a commotion, voices, one that didn't sound human, that only Aphrodite could make. In it was the high-pitched cry of fear and concern. Jordan turned back, and what she heard in the dolphin's voice she saw in his expression. Then his white face was fading, growing dim. A clear, hard bubble replaced it, was pressed down on her face. "Breathe it in, Lori, breathe it in!" As she did the pain in her chest eased, but now she became aware of a throbbing in her head. The rush of oxygen was pure heaven, but she was too exhausted to try to do as Jordan was begging. She was floating again on a sea of blackness. . . .

She opened her eyes, and the first thing that she saw was a metal pole with a plastic baggie-looking thing with water and bubbles in it. She saw Jordan bending over her, and the face of a woman with a white cap on her hair behind him.

"Head . . . hurts . . ." she whimpered.

Something wet daubed at her arm, and she felt a pinprick. She cried out and Jordan was saying, "Ssh, it'll stop the pain and help you sleep, Lori."

The woman—a nurse?—was murmuring something about when Lori woke she'd feel better, but everything was slipping away again, everything but a hand that held one of hers tightly, a lifeline that she clutched, and it followed her down into the blackness.

Peace. All was utter peace around Lori. She felt herself drifting in a great calm, as if she floated inside a large, fragile bubble. She opened her eyes and found why she drifted in such peace and tranquillity. Blue was all around, as if she floated in the midst of the sky. But it was the sea in which she floated, not the sky, the water as blue as the bluest cornflower and clear as purest crystal. Above, sunlight spilled down through the depths. Her hair streamed around her face, golden strands the color of the sunlight in the current. Looking down, Lori saw a grand building with walls of coral and tall, pointed buildings of clear amber and a roof of oyster shells that opened and closed in the tide, revealing glistening pearls.

Thinking she must be dreaming her favorite childhood fairy tale, the one by Hans Christian Andersen, Lori closed her eyes and then opened them again. She *was* a mermaid, a real scallop shell cupping each breast, her body ending in an emerald and sapphire tail, just as in the fairy story.

Other mermaids joined her, calling her sister, and they swam to sit at the knee of their grandmother, the Sea King's mother. She told them the story they loved best, of how when each girl was of age she would be allowed to rise to look at the other world above. Soon it would be Lori's turn, and she listened as each princess told of the time she had glimpsed something of the surface world. The oldest princess said that the nicest things she saw were the sights and sounds of the nearby town. Another said that the most beautiful sight was the sun going down into the water. The third sister spoke of children who could swim in the water when they had no tails. The fourth was not so bold, staying in the middle of the sea, where she watched dolphins leaping and great whales squirting water up through their blowholes like huge fountains, and there was nothing but sea for miles and miles around. The fifth sister's birthday was in the winter, and she talked of something the others had not seen: huge icebergs that looked like pearls and were quite lovely but whose sight appeared to frighten mortals who sailed in ships too close to them.

And then Lori was being told it was her turn to ascend to the surface. She swam toward the sunlight and broke the surface. The first thing she saw was a man standing on a ship, a man with dark hair and beautiful eyes. As she watched the man a storm blew up and the ship dived beneath the surface of the water like a swan, its sails billowing like wings beneath the waves. People fell into the water, and she looked for the handsome man, hoping that he would come down to her. But then she remembered that people could not live beneath the water, so she swam to save him, taking him to an island nearby where she cradled him in her arms, kissing him and breathing life into him. He came to life and somehow she was beneath him and he was kissing her and he was breathing for her.

The kiss of life became the kiss of passion and then of pain and she was fighting him off, pushing him aside and slipping back into the water. A dark shape pursued her, something dark and menacing, something that had Jordan's face and arms and the sleek gray form of a shark. When a mermaid died, she became foam upon the water and as he caught her and wrapped his arms around her, dragging her down, his mouth stealing all the breath from her, she felt her soul rise to the surface. . . .

Inexplicably she was human again, standing with Jordan amidst piles of foam lining the storm-splashed beach behind her apartment house. Jordan was saying he'd known he couldn't get a grant for her work, but he hadn't told her before they'd gone on the trip to the Keys because he didn't want to upset her. . . . She grew agitated, fighting his arms as he tried to hold her and talk to her. But she wouldn't listen, breaking free to run and run. Her feet splashed at the edge of the surf and foam flecked the hems of her jeans and she was falling into a watery void. This time it wasn't warm and pretty and tranquil as when she'd been the mermaid but cold and threatening. She floundered, breathing in water through her nose, fighting for air, fighting to make it to the surface.

She woke, bathed in a cold sweat, to find herself in a room she didn't recognize. A woman dressed in white came in and approached the bed, smiling as she saw that Lori was awake.

"How are you feeling?" she asked, immediately popping a thermometer into Lori's mouth, preventing her from answering. "Head feel better?"

Lori nodded.

"You sustained a concussion when you hit your head on the concrete beside a swimming pool."

Swimming pool? Lori was confused until she remembered she'd been beside Aphrodite's tank and the woman probably had just not gotten her facts straight. With the memory of the accident came others that had gotten tangled up, distorted in the dreams and nightmares Lori had been having because of the blow to her head and the drug she could remember another nurse giving her. What had happened to Jordan? He'd been in the room, soothing her when the shot had hurt and holding her hand as she fell back into unconsciousness. Had his presence here been a dream too?

The nurse caught Lori's searching glance around the room and smiled. "We kicked him out about an hour ago, sent him home to bed. Told him he'd scare you half to death if you woke up and saw him looking like he was."

The nurse took back her thermometer, studied the number now recorded upon it. When Lori opened her mouth to ask just what had been meant by the cryptic statement about how Jordan had looked, she was shushed while her pulse was taken.

"How did he look?" Lori asked when the woman finished.

"Who?"

"Jordan, the man who was here."

"Oh, him. Bleary-eyed and in need of a shave. Heard he sat here all yesterday afternoon and all last night since you were brought in. Actually he didn't sit, he was up and down, driving the night nurses crazy making them check you over and over again. It took quite a bit of effort to convince him you were going to be all right."

The doctor she usually saw once a year for checkups stopped by and confirmed that she had nothing to worry about, she'd be fine with a couple days rest in the hospital. When Lori protested, he conceded that she could rest just as well at home if she agreed to another night of observation here.

"Lori, are you really okay?" Betsy cried when she hurried into the room a few minutes later. "Ben, the night watchman, called me last night—Jordan told him to since we're friends. He was the only one allowed to see you. And they thought they were going to keep me out today," she said pointedly, glaring at the nurse, who came hard on her heels. The two, hands on hips, had a silent stand-off that the nurse managed to pretend she'd won by saying she'd heard someone calling her.

Betsy dropped her purse into the chair beside the bed and came over to place the back of her hand against Lori's forehead. "No fever."

"Betsy, they have people to do that."

"They're too busy throwing people like me out of the patients' rooms," the other woman said cheerfully as she moved her purse and settled in the chair. "Anyway, I promised to drop by Jordan's boat on the way to the office and tell him how you're doing. How's the head?"

"Don't ask," said Lori with a grimace. "It feels like it's going to come off if I move."

"Jordan asked me to tell his secretary to get someone to lay rubber or whatever around the tank so no one would ever have an accident like that again."

"The accident was my own fault; I was careless and not watching where I was walking."

"It can't hurt, just in case. The poor man was just about beside himself, from what Ben said. Jordan saw Aphrodite doing all kinds of flips in the tank and making a racket to get attention, and he realized something must be wrong. By the time he and Ben got there Aphrodite had you to the surface, but you weren't breathing. Ben said he was convinced you were dead; there was no telling how long you'd been under, and your face was gray and blood was running down it from where you'd hit your head. Jordan did mouth to mouth resuscitation on you until the ambulance Ben called got there. I—" At that point Betsy burst into tears and Lori had to comfort her and cheer *her* up, reassuring her friend that she only had a bump on the head and would be allowed to go home the next day.

Lori dozed after Betsy left, waking hopefully every time a nurse entered to take her temperature or give medication or bring flowers that had started to arrive from people at the facility who'd heard about her accident.

Lunch was chicken broth and lime gelatin and apple juice, just like breakfast; she was promised she'd be taken off the soft diet the doctor had prescribed at her next meal. There were visits from people she worked with and Betsy again. Betsy had the unfortunate luck to be in the room with two other visitors at the time her nemesis looked in, the nurse of that morning's glaring encounter. The nurse gave her a crocodile smile and told her she had to leave; only two visitors at a time, and since she'd been there once already that morning, she'd want the others to stay, right?

"In the words of MacArthur, 'I shall return,'" muttered Betsy as she hugged Lori before leaving. "Got your purse? Give me your apartment key and I'll bring you back a robe and nightie."

The man she'd hoped to see all that morning stood

in the door frame now, silent, unsmiling, dark eyes intent on her, as if drinking in the sight of her. He stayed there, made no move to enter the room. Finally, growing a little nervous, Lori asked, "Aren't you coming in?"

He nodded, strode inside. "I wasn't sure I'd be welcome."

"Why would you think . . ." she started to say, then stopped. He meant because of the argument. Now that he was closer, she could see faint circles beneath his eyes, evidence of the sleep he'd missed sitting in the chair beside this bed the night before. He was putting a box into her hands, saying, "I brought you this."

Lori opened the box and lifted out crumpled newsprint. "You brought me newspaper?" she questioned wryly, attempting to break the tension that hovered between them, heavy and omnipresent like the ache in her head. She saw him smile slightly as she gave her attention to lifting out the gift revealed when she removed a wad of paper.

"The florist was closed, so I stopped at the shell shop and bought you a piece of rose-colored coral for your shell collection," Jordan explained as he settled into the chair. He wore a navy cotton pullover shirt and a pair of jeans; she wondered if he'd gone into work at all that day.

The coral in her hands reminded her of their trip, and the argument they'd had when they returned. Lori felt tears burning at the back of her eyelids. She had to apologize, and not just because he'd probably saved her life yesterday.

"How are you feeling?" he asked, and she realized

175

she'd been unconsciously fingering the small gauze bandage taped to one side of her forehead.

"My head hurts a little," she admitted.

A nurse entered to make the hourly checks of temperature, blood pressure and pulse, necessary because of the concussion. She glanced sharply at Lori as she stuck the thermometer in her mouth, before Lori turned her head away from both the woman and Jordan. "Head bad?"

Lori nodded, glad of the excuse for the shine in her eyes, which the observant nurse had noticed.

The nurse frowned as she finished counting Lori's pulse and noted it on a piece of paper she returned to her pocket. Taking the thermometer, then scanning it, she turned to Jordan. "I think it'd be best if you could come back some other time. Her temp and pulse are up a bit, and she hasn't had much rest with all the visitors today."

Lori started to protest, but Jordan was standing, preparing to leave. He brushed the backs of his fingers along her cheek. "I'll see you later."

There was nothing for her to do but nod. His long strides carried him to the door. "Jordan?" He turned. "Thanks."

His glance went to the coral. "You're welcome." Then he was gone.

She hadn't been thanking him for the coral at all, but it was too late to call him back. Pills were brought for her headache, and she was grateful for the sleep that washed over her. She woke, feeling better, and was sitting up in bed, unenthusiastically stirring her dinner (stew, not soup this time; she'd been taken off the liquids she'd been on since she'd been admitted) when a figure clad in a trench coat slid around the door frame and edged inside her room. A head of bright red hair showed above the upturned collar. "Betsy?"

Flashing her a grin, Betsy lifted a forefinger to her lips. "Ssh! I told you I'd be back, didn't I? And I'm glad I did. You're sitting there just like the commercial on television with the little boy who's in bed with a cold and a tray on his lap, all alone, while his mommy's downstairs eating lunch with his little brother. Cheer up, kid!"

Watching as Betsy withdrew a thin square box from the tote bag she carried, Lori asked curiously, "Have you taken up spying for a hobby? Or are you dressed as one of the Marx brothers for a costume party?"

"Neither. I'm the pizza fairy, rescuing poor souls like you from hospital food." She moved the tray of food, wrinkling her nose as she did, and put the box on the table before Lori.

"I didn't know pizza fairies wore trench coats or carried tote bags."

"I didn't know you knew any other pizza fairies. The trench coat was a protective disguise in case Nurse Ratchet was around."

"Nurse Spann, and you'll be put in a 'cuckoo's nest' if anyone sees you dressed in a trench coat when it's this warm out."

After taking off the coat, Betsy took a slice of pizza and settled down into the chair. "Mmm. I know I'm no substitute for Jordan, but this isn't bad, is it?"

The pizza lost its taste. "No," she lied, attempting to swallow and finding it difficult around a lump in her throat that wasn't pizza.

"Oh, here, I forgot. I brought some soft drinks too."

"I thought you were on a diet."

"I am, but I skipped lunch, so it's okay."

Shaking her head and smiling at her logic—which Betsy knew herself always defeated her diets—Lori popped the tab on her soft drink.

"So, has Jordan been by?" At her friend's nod, Betsy said casually, "He told me about the fuss you two had about the grant."

"Oh?"

Betsy ignored her wary look and went on talking calmly around bites of pizza. "Yeah, I saw him at the facility this afternoon. He took me in his office and showed me letters he'd written, all the work he'd done to try to get us money for the project. He really believes in what you're doing, Lori. And in you."

"Did he send you over to try to get me to change my mind?"

"Hey, c'mon, you know me and you know Jordan. Would we try that?"

"As for you, absolutely," Lori told her with a grin.

"Right," Betsy agreed, grinning back. "And Jordan?"

"You have sauce on your chin."

Wiping it with a paper napkin, Betsy repeated encouragingly, "And Jordan? Would he try—or has he tried—to change your mind?"

Sighing, Lori put the slice of pizza down. "He's tried."

"Poor man. Didn't get anywhere, did he?" At Lori's sharp glance, she just laughed. "Hey, you're a doll and I love you, kid, but you gotta admit you're practically obsessive about the project. I hope you're not letting it get in the way of a relationship with Jordan because he had to cancel the project or because he's having trouble getting the grant?" Seeing Lori squirm, she was the one to sigh and put down her pizza now. "You didn't."

"I did."

Betsy got the whole story out of Lori—or most of it. Lori skipped over the time on Jordan's boat, but Betsy got the drift. "And even if I apologize, what good will it do? I'm not like you, Betsy, about men. . . ."

"Yeah, you've said that before, and I'm not sure I like the way you say it." Betsy pretended to be offended.

"No, you know what I mean!" Lori exclaimed, relieved when she saw her friend smile. "I see you happy when you're serious with a man and . . ." she trailed off, not sure how to explain it.

"And you don't feel that way with Jordan?"

"I did, for a while. Until—"

"Until you realized you loved him?"

"Yes." Her spirits rose. "How did you know?"

"I know you, remember?"

"So what *is* it with me?"

Betsy ran her finger around the top of the drink can as she thought about it. "I don't know. You're a warm, sweet girl. I know you can give love and receive it; I've seen that with the kids in the project and with Aphrodite and the other dolphins. With me and other people, sometimes you kind of—shy away from letting us get too close. Yeah, it's true," she said when Lori's eyes widened at the last part. "I always wondered if you had some kind of unhappy experiences with your parents. No?" she asked when Lori shook her head.

"You had foster parents, right? What about living with them? You've never told me much about your growing up."

"They were all great—Mom and Dad, even though I was little when they died, and Joe and Polly. They all just went away too soon," Lori said pensively. Her fingers smoothed the sheet that was pulled up to her waist over the hospital gown she wore. "Just when I really get someone to love like everybody else, they get snatched away." Betsy made a sound and she looked up. "What?"

"Did you hear what you said? Is that what you're afraid of, Lori? That you'll let yourself love someone and they'll be taken away?"

"I—"

"What is this, a pajama party?" inquired a nurse, entering the room, her bulk in a white uniform and high starched cap reminding Lori of a great ship with sails billowing in a strong wind. "Back again?" she asked Betsy. "Feet off the bed, young lady."

"Aw, Mom!" Betsy whined like a pouty teenager, taking her nylon-stockinged feet off the end of Lori's bed, where she'd propped them. "We were just having fun, jeez!"

The woman picked up the tray and went to exit the room. "I'll pretend I didn't see the pizza." She winked at Lori and started out.

"Thought she was off duty," Betsy whispered.

"Overtime!" they heard Nurse Spann say from just outside the door, where she was loading the tray on a cart.

Betsy kept Lori occupied for the next hour with her

lighthearted chatter, both of them pretending they didn't expect Jordan. But he was on both their minds. When Betsy went to leave at the end of visiting hours, she gave Lori a hug, saying, "Maybe it's better he didn't come until you figure out what you want. You can't be afraid of love, Lori, or you'll miss out on the best thing in life."

"Aristotle, right?"

"Nope, Betsy Pomeroy, the great philosopher of the ages. Call me when you're ready to go home tomorrow, hear?"

Lori lay on her side looking at the coral Jordan had given her, thinking about the conversation she'd had with Betsy. Was what they'd had during that trip to the Keys as dead as the coral? she asked herself. Only when the nurse came by with a sleeping pill hours later was Lori able to stop the endless soul-searching and rest.

Although Betsy as well as the Yamamotos had told her to call when she was discharged from the hospital, Lori thought it best to phone for a taxi and not disturb any of them at work. Thankfully Betsy had taken Lori's apartment key and on her second trip the previous day brought clothes for her to wear home.

The taxi passed the facility on the way home and impulsively Lori asked the driver to stop. She was afraid that she couldn't stand waiting for Jordan to come see her after he hadn't visited her again the evening before. And she was even more afraid that she might lose her nerve to talk to Jordan and see if she could make things right between them. . . .

The middle-aged taxi driver gave her a concerned

look. "I hope you're not going back to work so soon after getting out of the hospital, miss?"

She shook her head, smiling. "I'm just visiting someone; I won't be long."

"I can wait," he persisted. "I wouldn't want you to get to feeling bad and not have a way to get home."

In truth, Lori's legs were a little shaky, as if she'd just stepped back onto land after a long sea voyage, but she assured him that she was fine. She told him she had friends inside; she wouldn't be stranded. Betsy could always take her home if Jordan didn't want to do so.

To get to Jordan's office, Lori had to walk past Aphrodite's enclosure, and she decided to stop first to say hello to the dolphin. She found Jordan there too, standing with his back to her. The unexpectedness of seeing him there threw her off balance for a moment, and she backed away to retrace her steps and gather her courage.

"Lori! What are you doing here?"

"Hello, Jordan."

He closed the space between them and grasped her arms, his eyes searching her face. "What the hell can the doctor be thinking, letting you out so soon? You're pale and you look like a puff of air could blow you over. You should be in bed."

"I'm fine. I was on my way home, but I wanted to stop and . . ."

Jordan was releasing her, his face growing cold. "But you weren't coming to see me. It's just like last time; you were going to see Aphrodite and avoid me." There was a trace of bitterness in his voice. He sighed and took her hand, pulled her into the enclosure calling, "Aphrodite, look who's here! I told you she'd be all right, didn't I!"

This was going to be harder than she'd thought. "Hi, Aphrodite, I missed you so much!"

"Be careful!" Jordan said sharply as she approached the tank. "That's new," he said as she noticed the rubberized coating on the concrete edge, and she remembered Betsy telling her he'd ordered it installed. "I wanted to make sure no one got hurt again if they slipped."

Lori was careful as she sat down, and Aphrodite raised herself up onto her lap for a hug. Lori understood the sounds the dolphin made as ones giving and taking comfort and reassurance at the same time. "Thank you for helping me, girl," Lori told her, remembering what Betsy had said about Aphrodite's role in getting her to the surface of the tank that day and in alerting Jordan to the accident.

She glanced at Jordan. "I didn't get to say thank you for saving my life, too, before you had to leave the hospital room."

"You don't think I could have *not* done it, do you?"

Aphrodite slid from Lori's lap back into the tank, keeping her head and body vertical in the water. She regarded Lori with her dark, expressive eyes.

"No," Lori answered him softly. "But thank you all the same."

She stared at her hands, wishing she could remember all the words she'd rehearsed last night before she'd fallen asleep. It was as if the sleeping pill had erased them from her mind.

Aphrodite swam over to where Jordan stood and made a chirruping sound. He bent down and stroked her head. She left him, as if she hadn't really wanted his attention, returning to where Lori sat and flipping a spray of water at Lori with her nose.

"Aphrodite! Don't get her wet; she just got out of the hospital!" Jordan admonished.

Aphrodite was acting impatient with her. Why? she asked herself. "It's okay," she told Jordan, ignoring the drops of water dampening the knee of her jeans. "Maybe she's trying to tell me something."

Jordan glanced from her to Aphrodite; then he sighed. "Sometimes I wonder about you two. I get the feeling that if I could figure out one of you, I'd have the key to unlocking the mystery of the other."

Lori took a deep breath and plunged in. "Jordan, I want to apologize for making such a big deal about your not telling me about the grant before the trip. You were right; I was over-reacting. It wasn't fair of me, especially after you didn't get upset when I kept on with the project in spite of your wishes."

"Apology accepted," he said quietly. "Lori, about the grant. . . ."

She held up her hand. "No, please, let me finish. If you'd told me before the trip, we might never have gotten close. You were right about my blowing the whole thing out of proportion because I was afraid of what I was feeling for you." She paused. "Do you remember while we were on the trip how I told you about my parents and my foster parents?"

He nodded.

Lori looked at Aphrodite, who was glancing from one to the other, like a spectator at a tennis match. "I always thought my name was kind of ironic. Fairchild. I mean, I never was, really. Oh, I mean, I have blond hair and all, but the name sounds like someone . . . protected somehow, and I felt awfully vulnerable, lonely, as a child. And yet I was afraid to let anyone get close. I know it sounds crazy, but I lost one set of parents, then another couple who'd been like parents to me. I wasn't lucky with the one man I was serious about. I began to feel like there wasn't ever going to be anybody out there for me."

Jordan had been standing all the while they'd been talking, and she'd been half afraid he'd leave. Now he sat on the concrete near her. Lori began to hope that things could be worked out.

"I figured it was easier just not to need anyone and love them because it would hurt twice as bad if anything happened." Smiling wryly, she continued, "I've invented reasons to avoid you and run from you. I was afraid of you and my feelings and I've always seen myself as not afraid of anything. I even compared you to a shark in my mind."

"You weren't afraid of the one that went for you that day," he pointed out.

"I know. Crazy, huh? Only yesterday did I realize why I was afraid." She wrapped her arms around her knees, which were drawn up to her chest, and stared fixedly at Aphrodite, trying to absorb some of her steady calm. "And now I'm even more afraid," she said softly.

"Of what, Lori?"

"That you don't love me anymore."

"Lori, look at me." He caught and held her gaze with his. "I've never stopped loving you. Loving you is as necessary as breathing to me, and I have no intention of not doing either."

"And I love you."

Jordan was distracted by Aphrodite splashing water on the concrete near him. Then the dolphin was swimming over to Lori and doing the same near her. She splashed at each side of them again and again, and it became a game, forcing Jordan to move closer to Lori, and Lori closer to Jordan, until the two of them caught on. Lori was in his arms.

"Would you mind leaving us for a minute?" he asked Aphrodite. "I think we can handle it now."

The dolphin obligingly left them, swimming over to the other side of the tank.

Jordan grinned at Lori. "Will you marry me?"

"Do you need to ask? Can't you tell the answer to that?" she asked, her eyes shining as she smiled at him. "Look, she *knows*," she told him as Aphrodite appeared at their side again. The dolphin's smile had never appeared more angelic, wider, sweeter, more knowing. They both reached down to hug her.

Then Aphrodite was leaving them again, and Jordan and Lori didn't even miss her as they kissed and everything else faded away, everything but a breathless need for each other. She felt again the rapture she had that day when they had removed their air regulators beneath the sea and kissed and become a part of the beauty surrounding them, not even needing air.

"I haven't any breath left," she said with a shaky laugh when their mouths parted.

"Isn't it time you were tucked into bed for a rest?" he asked, standing and lifting her up into his arms.

"I think it's time I was tucked into it for *something*," she told him, smiling, and he laughed, calling her a brazen woman.

They said good-bye to Aphrodite, and then he was carrying her out of the enclosure, past several of the staff, who reacted as they had the last time something similar had happened: They gaped.

"Is this going to be a regular thing?" they heard someone ask.

"I sincerely hope so," Lori called over Jordan's shoulder, and she saw the smiles on everyone's faces. And then she gazed up at Jordan, and knew his love had put a smile to match Aphrodite's on her face.

YOU'LL BE SWEPT AWAY WITH SILHOUETTE DESIRE

$1.75 each

1 ☐ James   5 ☐ Baker   8 ☐ Dee

2 ☐ Monet   6 ☐ Mallory   9 ☐ Simms

3 ☐ Clay   7 ☐ St. Claire   10 ☐ Smith

4 ☐ Carey

$1.95 each

11 ☐ James	30 ☐ Lind	49 ☐ James	68 ☐ Browning
12 ☐ Palmer	31 ☐ James	50 ☐ Palmer	69 ☐ Carey
13 ☐ Wallace	32 ☐ Clay	51 ☐ Lind	70 ☐ Victor
14 ☐ Valley	33 ☐ Powers	52 ☐ Morgan	71 ☐ Joyce
15 ☐ Vernon	34 ☐ Milan	53 ☐ Joyce	72 ☐ Hart
16 ☐ Major	35 ☐ Major	54 ☐ Fulford	73 ☐ St. Clair
17 ☐ Simms	36 ☐ Summers	55 ☐ James	74 ☐ Douglass
18 ☐ Ross	37 ☐ James	56 ☐ Douglass	75 ☐ McKenna
19 ☐ James	38 ☐ Douglass	57 ☐ Michelle	76 ☐ Michelle
20 ☐ Allison	39 ☐ Monet	58 ☐ Mallory	77 ☐ Lowell
21 ☐ Baker	40 ☐ Mallory	59 ☐ Powers	78 ☐ Barber
22 ☐ Durant	41 ☐ St. Claire	60 ☐ Dennis	79 ☐ Simms
23 ☐ Sunshine	42 ☐ Stewart	61 ☐ Simms	80 ☐ Palmer
24 ☐ Baxter	43 ☐ Simms	62 ☐ Monet	81 ☐ Kennedy
25 ☐ James	44 ☐ West	63 ☐ Dee	82 ☐ Clay
26 ☐ Palmer	45 ☐ Clay	64 ☐ Milan	83 ☐ Chance
27 ☐ Conrad	46 ☐ Chance	65 ☐ Allison	84 ☐ Powers
28 ☐ Lovan	47 ☐ Michelle	66 ☐ Langtry	85 ☐ James
29 ☐ Michelle	48 ☐ Powers	67 ☐ James	86 ☐ Malek

Silhouette Desire

$1.95 each

87 ☐ Michelle	106 ☐ Michelle	125 ☐ Caimi	144 ☐ Evans
88 ☐ Trevor	107 ☐ Chance	126 ☐ Carey	145 ☐ James
89 ☐ Ross	108 ☐ Gladstone	127 ☐ James	146 ☐ Knight
90 ☐ Roszel	109 ☐ Simms	128 ☐ Michelle	147 ☐ Scott
91 ☐ Browning	110 ☐ Palmer	129 ☐ Bishop	148 ☐ Powers
92 ☐ Carey	111 ☐ Browning	130 ☐ Blair	149 ☐ Galt
93 ☐ Berk	112 ☐ Nicole	131 ☐ Larson	150 ☐ Simms
94 ☐ Robbins	113 ☐ Cresswell	132 ☐ McCoy	151 ☐ Major
95 ☐ Summers	114 ☐ Ross	133 ☐ Monet	152 ☐ Michelle
96 ☐ Milan	115 ☐ James	134 ☐ McKenna	153 ☐ Milan
97 ☐ James	116 ☐ Joyce	135 ☐ Charlton	154 ☐ Berk
98 ☐ Joyce	117 ☐ Powers	136 ☐ Martel	155 ☐ Ross
99 ☐ Major	118 ☐ Milan	137 ☐ Ross	156 ☐ Corbett
100 ☐ Howard	119 ☐ John	138 ☐ Chase	157 ☐ Palmer
101 ☐ Morgan	120 ☐ Clay	139 ☐ St. Claire	158 ☐ Cameron
102 ☐ Palmer	121 ☐ Browning	140 ☐ Joyce	159 ☐ St. George
103 ☐ James	122 ☐ Trent	141 ☐ Morgan	160 ☐ McIntyre
104 ☐ Chase	123 ☐ Paige	142 ☐ Nicole	161 ☐ Nicole
105 ☐ Blair	124 ☐ St. George	143 ☐ Allison	162 ☐ Horton

SILHOUETTE DESIRE, Department SD/6
1230 Avenue of the Americas
New York, NY 10020

Please send me the books I have checked above. I am enclosing $_____
(please add 75¢ to cover postage and handling. NYS and NYC residents please
add appropriate sales tax). Send check or money order—no cash or C.O.D.'s
please. Allow six weeks for delivery.

NAME_____

ADDRESS_____

CITY_____ STATE/ZIP_____

For the woman who expects a little more out of love, get Silhouette Special Edition.

Take 4 books free – no strings attached.

If you yearn to experience more passion and pleasure in your romance reading ... to share even the most private moments of romance and sensual love between spirited heroines and their ardent lovers, then Silhouette Special Edition has everything you've been looking for.

Get 6 books each month before they are available anywhere else!

Act now and we'll send you four exciting Silhouette Special Edition romance novels. They're our gift to introduce you to our convenient home subscription service. Every month, we'll send you six new passion-filled Special Edition books. Look them over for 15 days. If you keep them, pay just $11.70 for all six. Or return them at no charge.

We'll mail your books to you *two full months before they are available* anywhere else. Plus, with every shipment, you'll receive the Silhouette Books Newsletter absolutely free. *And with Silhouette Special Edition there are never any shipping or handling charges.*

Mail the coupon today to get your four free books — and more romance than you ever bargained for.

Silhouette Special Edition is a service mark and a registered trademark of Simon & Schuster, Inc.

MAIL COUPON TODAY

Silhouette Special Edition®
120 Brighton Road, P.O. Box 5020, Clifton, N. J. 07015

☐ Yes, please send me FREE and without obligation, 4 exciting Silhouette Special Edition romance novels. Unless you hear from me after I receive my 4 FREE BOOKS, please send me 6 new books to preview each month. I understand that you will bill me just $1.95 each for a total of $11.70 — with no additional shipping, handling or other charges. **There is no minimum number of books that I must buy, and I can cancel anytime I wish.** The first 4 books are mine to keep, even if I never take a single additional book.

BSD9R4

☐ Mrs.   ☐ Miss   ☐ Ms.   ☐ Mr.

Name	(please print)	
Address		Apt. No.
City	State	Zip

Signature (If under 18, parent or guardian must sign.)

This offer, limited to one per customer, expires March 31, 1985. Terms and prices subject to change. Your enrollment is subject to acceptance by Simon & Schuster Enterprises.